# Forever Romances

# MORNING SONG

*Linda Timian Herring*

**Forever ❧ Romances**

is an imprint of
Guideposts Associates, Inc.
Carmel, NY 10512

*To Bea, who planted,*
*To Mel, who watered,*
*To Mom and Dad and the rest of the family,*
*    who helped with the harvest,*
*And to Anne, who provided the yeast,*
*My love and thanks.*

# CHAPTER 1

THE HOT EAST TEXAS sunlight slipped gently through the colors of the stained-glass window, putting fire in the ruby reds and ice in the cobalt blues. Carole Morgan sat tensed in a pew under the brilliant windows, the colors accentuating her dark auburn hair and smoky blue eyes.

Those eyes were riveted on the distinguished-looking man speaking from the ornate pulpit. Rev. Daniel Thornton's own deep brown gaze swept the congregation as he spoke. She clung to his words as a drowning person clutches debris, for his presence had carried her back in time.

Had Samuel really been dead five years? The thought startled her. Five years since that terrible day when Daniel Thornton had buried her minister husband.

Memories of the days after Samuel's death kept springing into her head. She had been truly almost as dead as Samuel. The only thing that had kept her moving back toward life was Daniel Thornton, and the comfort of God's words that he brought to her. He knew her grief first-hand, for he had buried his wife only the year before. How Carole had leaned on him for support. And how she had missed that support when she moved from the parsonage to another city. The widow of a pastor must move on to make room for the new minister and his wife. And so Carole chose to move to Longview to start all over, and the years had slipped by.

Once again she listened carefully to the words he spoke in that deep, melodic voice, and found strength as he preached the Word of God to an attentive audience.

Daniel Thornton was a commanding presence in the pulpit. The Scriptures sprang to life with new clarity and meaning under his interpretation. But even as his preaching reached the peak of intensity, Carole noticed the curly lock of dark brown hair that fell over his forehead and the trim, muscular body, taut with purpose. Above the white surplice his earnest face, deeply tanned, bore an expression of deep concern for his new flock.

She glanced casually around her. The church was full, forcing a few latecomers to find standing room at the back. Most of the women were smiling slightly, their faces betraying, like Carole's, their errant thoughts. They were obviously enjoying the view, too. A nice change from the rotund Rev. Sanders.

Carole was delighted when she learned that Daniel was coming to Longview to be the new pastor. He had been one of Samuel's seminary buddies, and she knew him, if only casually. She knew, too, that Daniel would be a strong leader and a good example for the people.

Reluctantly she forced her mind back to the sermon, only to find that the service was coming to a close. As Rev. Thornton raised his arms in the final benediction, the sleeves of his surplice floated out like great white birds.

As she moved down the aisle in the line waiting to shake hands with the new pastor, Carole felt nervous. She never dreamed that seeing him again would have such a powerful effect on her. *Will he still remember me?* He has taken care of so many people since Samuel's death. And then she was annoyed with herself. *I'm acting like a thirteen-year-old girl. What difference does it make whether he remembers or not?* Keeping that thought firmly in mind she moved along, chatting with the people around her, while the organ sounded the triumphant strains of "Trumpet Volentare."

"Hello, Pastor Thornton. Your first sermon here was most thought-provoking," she said in a voice that sounded quite calm in contrast to the quickening pace of her heartbeat.

"Carole! Carole Morgan! I've wondered where you moved. I should have known I'd find you in church."

"Well, of course," she laughed. "Even though my days as Mrs. Pastor are over, I'm still very much involved. It is nice, though, just being part of the congregation. I don't miss all those extra responsibilities."

He was smiling and nodding at her, and then he said smoothly as he let go of her hand and turned to greet another parishioner, "Let's have lunch sometime soon."

"Certainly," she responded brightly, and cringed inwardly at being so blunt about not missing a life he obviously thought was wonderful. *You silly goose,* she chastised herself as she walked out of the church into the August heat.

The heavy, sultry air took her breath away after the conditioned air of the church. There wasn't a hint of a breeze to cool the slight blush on Carole's delicately molded cheeks. She could feel the full sun on her body, so she stepped into the delicious shade of the tall pine that guarded the walkway. She never tired of looking at those pines. Coming as she did from the treeless Panhandle, it was heavenly.

The white brick church was set on the crest of a heavily wooded hill, its tapering spire a lofty symbol that could be seen for miles. White columns marched evenly across the front of the church, and the windows that graced the sides of the large building told their stories in beautiful panes of colored glass. The road wound its way down to a busy street below. Carole was enchanted to find this jewel tucked away in the heart of a busy city. It was a promise of serenity and peace in the middle of the busyness of her life.

After briefly visiting with several friends, she walked briskly to her little white sports car. Adjusting the rear-view mirror, she noticed that her cheeks were still gently rosy and she idly wondered if it were her chagrin . . . or the Rev. Daniel Thornton.

As she drove up the street to her home, she felt again the pleasure of having a place of her own—a joy long denied her as a minister's wife. In the interest of economy, parsonages were usually provided for the pastor and his family. Now that Carole was alone, she had chosen to live in an older part of the city where the trees and houses had endured together, growing more dignified with age. She didn't need a large home, opting instead for a smaller one, but she was glad once again that she had spared no expense in decorating tastefully and in hiring a yardman to keep the spacious grounds carefully manicured.

She unlocked the heavy wooden front door and stepped into the elegant entrance hall. Her high-heeled shoes clicked on the pale terrazzo tiles as she walked to the gilded French table with large matching mirror. She dropped her keys on the marble top and walked by the doorway to the formal living room and on through the comfortable den, then slipped off her shoes and felt the deep plush carpet under her bare feet. Dangling the shoes from her fingers, she walked down the hallway to her bedroom.

This room above all the others was where she had concentrated her time and skill. The walls were a pale shade of blue, setting off the deep piled blue, gray, and white carpeting. Softly curved French furniture lent a distinctly feminine air. Each time Carole entered this lovely sanctuary, she felt completely at ease. Blue was a soothing color for her and smoothed the rough edges of her active days.

She pushed open the tiny-paned French doors and walked barefoot into a walled garden, where an old magnolia tree shaded one portion of the small garden and made it invitingly cool. In the mornings she could sunbathe in privacy if she wished. She often did on Saturdays, feeling deliciously sensuous as the sun poured over her body.

She went back into her bedroom to change into a pair of shorts. In front of the mirror, she examined her full-length reflection with a critical eye. Lustrous shoulder-length auburn hair framed a heart-shaped face and soft winglike brows accented her dark blue eyes. She hated her nose; it was narrow and slightly tipped. *Some day I'll get rid of that tip*, she promised herself. Her mouth was full and mobile and smiled easily. She pirouetted in front of the mirror and noted her body kept trim and supple with regular tennis and swimming.

Lunch with Daniel Thornton might be interesting . . .

He didn't call her for lunch as he promised. The days sped by, filled with the challenges of her job as a vice president at the bank. Carole enjoyed helping people solve their financial problems and habitually arrived at the bank early, a practice that gave her time to review the folders of customers she would be seeing later in the day.

"Good morning, Mrs. Morgan," her secretary said crisply. She brought Carole the morning mail. "Will you be eating in the Executive Dining Room for lunch today?"

"Yes, Sandy, luncheon as usual. Mr. Whitaker has several new proposals for our expansion branch in the new mall. It will be interesting to see how they plan to put in a miniature bank that's totally automated." Her merry smile did indeed indicate that the idea was not only interesting but exciting.

The soft pleated lilac jersey dress Carole was wearing was a favorite and she was aware that it deepened the auburn color of her hair and showed off her figure to good advantage. Sitting down at her desk, she waited patiently for Sandy to give her a run-down of the day's activities. At the end of a lengthy recital, she laughingly asked, "Is that all?"

"I'll see if I can line up a ground-breaking and a grand opening, if you're afraid you'll be bored today." She grinned impishly.

"Thanks a bunch." She shooed Sandy out of her office and tackled the first in a large stack of papers on her desk. Stopping only to take the telephone calls that Sandy screened for her, she was able to get a fair amount of paperwork done.

Carole's office was more efficient-looking than plush, she thought, as she looked around with satisfaction. It had the businesslike air of decision-making that changed people's lives. Perhaps it was the chrome and dark brown leather of the handsome furnishings. The only concession to femininity was a lead crystal bud vase cradling a single yellow rosebud on her huge pecan-paneled desk.

At ten-thirty a discreet knock on the door signaled that Sandy was bringing in steamy rich coffee for her morning break. As Carole sipped the fragrant brew, she opened one of her desk drawers and withdrew Sunday's church bulletin casually. Reading the words *Pastor, Daniel Thornton,* she felt a tingle ruffle the hair at the nape of her neck. Ruefully she realized it was already Wednesday and there had as yet been no call.

"Deep in your heart you know you'd run like a rabbit from a coyote if he made a move toward you." Speaking the words aloud had the effect of making them more real. Her life now was infinitely less demanding and structured. Finally she was an individual, not just an extension of her husband. Not Mrs. Pastor—a package deal.

She knew the wisdom and truth of these words and sighed a deep sigh of regret. Glancing over the calendar of activities at the church, she noted an evening meeting she really should attend. Straightening her shoulders and her will, however, she resolved not to go. She jotted a memo to Sandy, instructing her to phone Daniel, informing him that her crowded schedule would not permit her attendance. As if to verify this, her phone rang, bringing an end to her reverie.

"Carole, this is Daniel Thornton." The deep, resonant voice caused her to drop the memo in surprise.

"I was just going to have my secretary call you," she said, flustered.

"Too busy to do it yourself?" He seemed more amused than insulted.

"Well, no," she stalled guiltily. "I was just afraid you might be hard to reach and . . ." She trailed off her part of the conversation.

"I'm sure it's too late to ask you for dinner this evening, but how about a cup of coffee after the meeting tonight? We'll be needing it after doing the groundwork for next year's budget. That usually takes all the starch out of me."

The heartiness in his voice made her smile. But it was the underlying request for her company to speed his recovery from the rigors of the meeting that struck just the right chord in her to elicit a positive response.

"Well . . . all right," she conceded. "Where shall I meet you?"

"Meet me? I thought we could just leave together after the meeting. You *are* coming, aren't you?" He sounded disappointed.

"Oh, well, yes, of—of course," she stammered.

"Good," he said. "See you at the meeting. Then we'll have a chat and catch up on the years in between. Bye."

"Bye?—" She fumbled for the proper term of address. *Pastor Thornton? Pastor? Daniel?* None of them felt comfortable, so she weakly echoed, "Bye," and hung up.

As she leaned back in her chair, she felt that tingle at the nape of her neck again. But the soft smile in her eyes and her mouth made it clear that it was not an unpleasant sensation. She pressed the buzzer of the intercom.

"Sandy, I'll be leaving at six-thirty this evening. Get everything wrapped up for me by then." *Well, after all,* she thought, *I will need some time to change from secular to sacred thinking, and perhaps time for a quick bath before dinner.* She scooped some papers into a smart leather case and paused, a tiny frown creasing her smooth forehead. *What in the world am I getting myself into!*

Since Carole would be leaving the church with Daniel after the meeting, she decided to take a cab to the church. With her butterflies somewhat settled, she noted the number of cars parked in front of the Annex as she wound up the long drive promptly at seven-fifteen. *Good turn-out,* she thought as she stepped from the cab. Yet she knew from experience that the reasons for the good attendance would be as varied as the people themselves. It might mean strong support for the pastor and the budget, or it might mean equally strong opposition. In either case, it usually meant a lot of discussion.

She heard footsteps behind her and turned to see a heavy, red-faced man and a matching woman.

"Good evening, Carole," said the Millers in unison. By reputation, they were known as constant complainers, for whom nothing was ever satisfactory. Carole automatically responded politely—but without enthusiasm.

Among themselves clergymen jokingly referred to these people as "carriers."

Carole had first heard the term from Jeremiah Brown at a ministers' conference. "They never have ulcers, but they're carriers. They give 'em to us!" And though it was said in jest, each man knew just what he meant. It was an occupational hazard rarely mentioned in the ivory towers of the seminary.

"Oh, I don't mind," replied another minister. "They're so negative about everything that the moment they get up to speak, the entire voting body will vote yes just to shut them up. Passed a lot of programs that way. I've gotten quite fond of my carriers. Feel a little sorry for them, too. They'll never change. Probably be arguing with Saint Peter at the gates of heaven about who ought to have access to the keys." And each man chuckled, recognizing his own "carrier."

As she walked into the room, Carole saw that the Johnsons were already there—a dedicated young couple. And George Williams, one of the most respected parish members, and chairman of the committee. There were several others whom Carole didn't recognize. But it only took a second to spot her friend Joyce's smiling face.

Though Joyce was single and shared few of Carole's life experiences, their friendship had been forged only moments after meeting. Joyce had served on virtually every committee of the church at one time or another and was a veritable library of church information.

Then Daniel arrived, greeting everyone cheerfully. Even the Millers were included in his genial welcome. He smiled broadly when he spotted Carole, but made no special effort to sit beside her. Her casual reply matched his, but she couldn't help feeling a special warmth as she thought about the time to come when the meeting was over. It would be good to visit with him after these years. The harmonious atmosphere lasted throughout the opening prayer and the reading of the minutes.

"Any corrections or additions?" asked George. He recognized a slightly balding, middle-aged man.

"Well, that special service was held on the fifteenth, not the fourteenth," the man drawled.

"So noted. Any other corrections?" He paused and looked around the table. "Then the minutes stand approved as corrected." George flipped a page of the notebook on the table in front of him. Carole felt a muscle in her stomach contract slightly as she looked down and across the table where Daniel was sitting. She knew the unfinished business on the agenda would be his proposed salary raise.

Daniel looked calm and dignified. He nodded optimistically to Carole, and she smiled back encouragingly.

guess everyone knows the next item on the agenda. The Board of Elders has recommended a 4 percent raise for Pastor Thornton this year." George smiled approvingly at Daniel.

"I move we accept the recommendation of the elders," said an earnest Mrs. Johnson.

George recognized Mr. Miller with just a hint of the inevitable in his voice.

"Well, now, I hate to bring up an unpleasant subject, but let's be realistic about this. Attendance is down and the offerings have been off the last few months." His tone was laced with accusations.

Daniel's expression did not change.

Mel Johnson didn't wait to be recognized. "In the sum-

16

mertime, attendance and offerings are always a little off."
Mel spoke earnestly. "That doesn't mean our pastor doesn't
deserve a raise for all the work he does all year long. We
can't force people to come to church," he added defensively.

Miller's retort was swift. "Well, maybe his sermons need
to be a lot more law and a lot less gospel. Put the fear into
them, so to speak."

Daniel's face was slightly flushed and his eyes averted as
the discussion flowed around him.

George spoke in a conciliatory manner. "Perhaps we
need to be reminded that this raise has nothing to do with
evaluating the work of the pastor. This raise is to bring us in
line with the District's suggested salary scale and cost of
living increase. It was a recommendation made even before
Pastor Thornton got here."

"I still say he should earn it," snapped Miller.

Carole's color deepened, too, but her eyes were flashing
as she bit her tongue. Years of practice in the art of restraint
kept her from unleashing a few well-remembered thunder-
bolts. She wanted to run from the room, away from the
ugliness, but she knew Daniel needed her vote. She locked
knowing eyes with Joyce, and just as Mr. Miller was about
to launch into the excesses of medical coverage and pen-
sions, she satisfied her need to speak by calling for the
question. The raise passed.

"There is one more item on the agenda," George said,
leaning back in his chair. "We need two lay representatives
for the district convention."

There was a sudden dropping of eyes and perusal of perfectly manicured nails. Daniel scanned the faces around the
room for a look of interest. One or two were overheard to
say, ". . . but there is no way I can get away for three
days."

"Joyce and I will be happy to go," Carole volunteered, darting a glance at her friend. "Conventions are fun, and this one is so close. It's only a three-hour drive to Dallas. Now, what were those dates again?" She could hear the wheels turning in Joyce's head.

The atmosphere lightened considerably. The two most important items on the agenda had been resolved with a minimum of bloodshed.

Carole was relieved when Daniel closed the meeting with a thoughtful prayer and bid each member an impartially friendly good night. She wished he would rush a bit, both dreading and anticipating the evening ahead, and was glad when he finally took her arm and steered her toward the door. Carole turned toward Joyce and waved a tiny, discreet good-by as she and Daniel left the room together. *I wish I had a camera,* she thought. The incredulous look on Joyce's face was priceless.

Daniel opened the door for Carole and then settled into the seat, breathing a deep sigh of relief. "Well, that really wasn't so bad tonight."

"Pastor, you're lying," she challenged him boldly.

"Please, Carole, forget the formality. Call me Daniel," he pleaded, grinning. "We went through some hard times together. And the meeting really *wasn't* so bad. I've had much, much worse."

As Carole looked into those mockingly somber eyes, she confessed shyly, "I wasn't sure how familiar I should be with you—Daniel. It was you and Samuel who were best friends in seminary. I didn't know you very well—and it's been a long time since—" His searching look told her he hadn't forgotten their shared experience of grief.

"I really prefer being called by my first name by the members of my congregation. I hope it makes me more human to them, and less of a target. Sitting up high on a pedestal can not only be lonely—it can be downright dangerous," he laughed.

"I know. I was a target for a lot of years myself," she replied, a trace of bitterness in her voice.

"I know you don't miss that part, but don't you ever miss the good times?"

"Oh, yes, especially the 'honeymoon' period—when you first get to a place. Everyone wants to be your friend, particularly the ones who were on the outside circle with the last pastor."

"That sounds a bit calloused," he said, lifting his eyebrows in surprise.

"Oh, after a while you get to really know the people and choose your own friends. Of course, that can get you into trouble, too." There was no mistaking the sarcasm of this statement.

His handsome brow was furrowed as he started the car down the winding, dark road.

"You had a pretty rough time when you were married to Sam." It was more a statement than a question.

"Oh, the usual good with the bad," she replied matter-of-factly.

"I think there were some very hard times." He looked at her quizzically.

Carole ignored the opening. "Let's just say I'm not overly eager to resurrect my former sainthood." She lavished a convincing smile on him.

He took his cue and changed the subject for the rest of their ride to the restaurant.

When they arrived they found several of Daniel's parish members already seated at a large table. Chairs were added to make room for the couple at the far end, affording them a certain amount of privacy. But it was impossible not to be swept up in the mood of the crowd. The music was soft and dreamy; the candlelight sent flickering shadows dancing on the walls. The atmosphere worked its soothing magic, and Carole felt herself relaxing in spite of her earlier apprehension. Even Daniel seemed different here—all traces of strain disappearing from his strong-jawed face.

Leaning toward her, he said softly, "Hey, lady, I'm glad you came with me."

She felt a little breathless at his proximity. The rough weave of his jacket resting alongside her bare arm on the table was disconcerting, and she tried desperately not to think of his long legs under the table brushing innocently against her slender ones. The scent of his musky cologne sent a shiver through her, and she suddenly had trouble lifting her water glass to her trembling lips.

Again he spoke. "Having a good time?" At her nod, he added, "You look lovely in the moonlight."

"We're not in the moonlight." Laughter lit her eyes.

"If we were, you'd look lovely in it," he responded gallantly, without a trace of mockery in his smile.

"You handled yourself very well at the meeting tonight. Grace under fire, and all that," she offered in an attempt to cover her confusion.

"Oh, I always *think* I'm well prepared for those budget meetings. The same thing happens every time. Yet, I still get caught off guard when I'm hit with some blatant criticism. You'd think my skin would be like an elephant's hide after so many years," he sighed. "I preach love and gentleness—building each other up. You heard the other people defending me, but that one sour note sticks in my mind and I hear it played over and over again. There's always that nagging doubt that maybe, just maybe, he's right." That doubt was plainly reflected in his troubled eyes.

"Daniel, you're your own worst critic," she scolded gently. "I used to hear this same thing after each budget meeting. Money seems to bring out the worst in some Christians."

He smiled a little tiredly. "Yup. It's one of Satan's best tools." Her smile encouraged him to go on. "Just about this time every year I decide that maybe I should have been a plumber."

"You would still be working with other people's problems," she reminded him.

"Maybe so, but I wouldn't have to go to budget meetings," he quipped.

"But you might still have to get to the root of the problem."

"Oh, Carole, that's a terrible pun," he complained.

"Seriously, Daniel, why don't you fight back when someone attacks you like that?" Her brows furrowed with her concern.

"Oh, I could probably chop old Miller up fairly well, but I prefer to practice what I preach—corny as that might sound. I just wait to see if anyone will defend me. Someone usually does."

With flashing eyes, Carole sputtered, "Well, it just isn't fair. You make such a big target. It makes me want to scratch out his eyes."

"I see you prefer the direct approach. Remind me not to make you mad at me." His impish grin caused her to laugh in spite of the unexpected anger she felt.

"I'm sorry I got so angry." She was instantly contrite. "Guess I'm not a good example, either."

"Those tiny little roses in your cheeks tell me you are truly repentant, my child. *Pax vobiscum.*"

"I shall go in peace, and thank-you, Father O'Malley. You know, for a priest, you've a glib tongue. I feel sorry for the nuns in the convent next door. You could probably talk them into almost anything."

"Ah, Sister, me shirts do need a bit of the needle." His eyes danced in merriment.

"That's the worst Barrymore I've ever heard," she said. But the gaiety in her smile belied her words.

"You know, Carole, you're so nice to talk to. I feel perfectly relaxed with you." Just the tiniest bit of color highlighted his strong cheekbones. "Well, you know what I mean. I needed this."

"Me, too."

Some of the couples at the table began to move about, gathering up their things. One of Daniel's members leaned across the table and grinned wickedly, "Sure was nice talking to you two." Carole and Daniel looked at each other sheepishly and rose hurriedly to leave with the others.

The ride to Carole's house was marked with general conversation and easy silences. When they arrived, Daniel walked her to the door.

"I had a lovely time." She inserted her key in the lock and swung the door open.

"So did I. It's been awhile since I've felt so thoroughly at ease with a woman. Usually I feel I'm being measured as possible husband material. It's nice just to relax with you. Let's do this again soon, Carole." His face reflected the sincerity of his words.

She put out her hand in a formal gesture. "Thank-you, Daniel."

He took her hand in both of his. "Good night."

Turning, Carole walked into the hallway. She closed the door softly and leaned against it for an instant. Then, dropping her purse on the table, she took off her shoes and whirled her way around and around down to her bedroom.

She caught a glimpse of her reflection in the dressing table mirror—the luminous eyes, the high color in her cheeks, the laughing mouth. She stopped dead still and stared.

"What are you doing, you idiot!" she said aloud. "Look at you. Dancing around like a woman possessed." Moving closer to the mirror, she talked directly to her mirrored image. She spoke slowly and distinctly. "He is a minister, remember? Minister. As in—we left all that behind us. No more. Never again. A little conversation and laughter, and you're acting like a grade-A dope. Have you forgotten the little old ladies who liked to tell you what to wear? Or the hateful men like Miller who lacerated your heart? Careful, now. Remember. Remember."

She went to bed angry, but she wasn't sure if she were angry with Daniel Thornton for being a pastor, or herself for enjoying his company so much.

# CHAPTER 2

INSISTENT SUNLIGHT RACING from the French door to her pillow awakened Carole the next morning. She snuggled down deeper into the covers only to have her clock radio click on. She had gone to bed angry and she woke up angry. The disc jockey with his cheerful patter was the first victim of her ugly mood. She shut him off in mid-sentence with a swift finger, but not before he told her the time. She groaned at the unjustness of the hour, though normally she was an early riser, and struggled out of the warmth of her bed.

Dragging her dark clouds with her to the kitchen, she started the coffee. She scowled at the cheerful room, painted in sunburst yellow, but it couldn't begin to penetrate her gloom today. She poured the fresh coffee into an equally cheerful yellow mug. She stopped after pouring only half a cup and said gruffly to no one in particular, "I hate yellow mugs!" and took down a somber dark brown one from the cabinet. She felt a little better after repouring the coffee into the less offensive earth-colored mug. Nothing and nobody were going to force her to be happy this morning. Carrying the coffee cup with her, she headed for her bathroom and a warm bath.

Carole hoarded her anger like a miser, daring anyone or anything to make her spend it. She pinned up her heavy dark red-brown hair, and slid into the tub until the water touched her chin. Lying back on the warm slope of the tub, she surveyed her kingdom and talked to herself like a friend giving advice. "Life is a hard teacher, and you never ever learn it all. You've had to learn a lesson all over again. I thought you'd put away those rose-colored glasses a long time ago, my friend. Sometimes I don't think you're ever going to grow up." The next part of her lecture was delivered sternly. Her voice grew resolute, and her eyes a colder, harder blue. "And as for Daniel Thornton, you can just forget him. He's a minister, and the last man on earth you'd want to get involved with."

After making the decision to eliminate this potential troublemaker from her world, she felt better. A small grin lifted the corners of her lush mouth, and the restorative powers of her heart-to-heart talk, along with the warm bath, gave her a surge of energy. Buffing her skin to a golden sheen with a fluffy towel, she wrapped it around herself before padding back to the kitchen for that second cup of coffee. This time she used the bright yellow mug she had earlier rejected.

When Carole's phone rang Thursday evening, she wasn't surprised to hear Daniel's voice. She knew he'd call again, and she was totally prepared to keep him at arm's length now that she had talked it out with herself. She would be pleasant and charming, and just a little bit distant.

"Hello there. Is this the lady who rebuilds sagging egos? Hey, I just happen to know this great place that's opening this weekend. Want to help me show the people some real style?"

"My goodness," she countered, "is this the famous Cardinal Pushing?"

His groan was audible over the phone. "Honestly, Carole, you've got to quit those awful jokes. It's bad for your image as an intellectual."

"Oh, do I have that image?" Was there a tiny bit of frost in her remark?

"Hey, this is a friendly call. I didn't call to spar with you. I'd like to take a pretty lady to dinner. Will you go with me?" The honesty in his voice caused her to cringe at her abrasiveness.

"I'm sorry. I had a bad day at the bank. But I didn't mean to take it out on you." She hoped that the lies she was telling filtered through the telephone as truth. "Of course, I'd love to go with you."

"Good, I'll pick you up at eight." He signed off with a cheery "Good-by."

Now all she had to do was remember the nice little pep talk about how to have a good time without getting involved. A little fun never hurt anyone. She was pleased with the way she had handled the situation.


Friday evening came quickly, and Carole found herself humming as she dressed for her date. She slipped the smoky gray chiffon cloud over her shining hair, stepped into jeweled high-heeled sandals, then paused to check her appearance in the full-length mirror. *It's been so long,* she thought, *so long since I've dressed up, since I've felt this alive.* Tiny straps of gray pearls skimmed her shoulders and crossed in the back. The effect was startling—demure, yet warmly feminine. She nodded in approval, picked up the wisp of matching fabric that served as a light wrap, and left the room.

Daniel was prompt and dressed appropriately in a dark suit and tie. His boyish face was even more handsome than she remembered.

"Well, I can see you're ready." He smiled his appreciation. "So, since we have reservations right away, we ought to be leaving." Instead of hurrying her, however, he stood there, beaming at her and staring until she broke the silence.

"Is something wrong?"

"I've never seen you look so beautiful." The simplicity of his words revealed the depth of his feeling.

"Thank-you." Her answer was without affectation. Taking her evening purse from the gilded table, Carole floated out the door.

Daniel put her into the car the way a jeweler would carefully slip a Cartier diamond into its blue velvet case. Then he settled behind the wheel and the engine hummed to life.

Weaving the car deftly through the traffic, he said, "You know, I feel like a senior taking the prettiest girl in the class to the prom."

"You say the nicest things." Her voice was light, detached. "I'm looking forward to seeing this new place."

"Even with reservations, we may have a wait. The place will probably be packed. Later on we can always brag about how we were there for the opening."

"Do you think we'll see any of the congregation tonight?"

"Probably."

"Won't they—well, aren't you afraid they won't approve of your being there?"

He looked at her curiously, "I'm not doing anything I shouldn't be doing. It's a nice place—superb food, excellent music. If I shouldn't be there, they shouldn't be there,

27

either. Are you afraid they'll talk about my choice of recreation, or about *us?*"

"Both, I guess. You know how people love to talk about the pastor."

"You worry too much about what other people will think. You can't live the way you think people expect you to live. You could drive yourself crazy trying to please everyone. I can see you need some serious tutoring in 'Having Fun 101.' Don't worry, Carole, I won't compromise your reputation or your morals."

When he put it that way, she felt foolish for even asking the question. But her early experiences had taught her to lead a circumspect life, never giving anyone the slightest cause for complaint. Her lips were a little stiff as she said, "We were talking about *your* life. I'm a civilian now."

"Sorry if I hit a raw nerve." His expression was contrite. "I just want you to have a good time. Okay?"

"All right." She turned her face slightly toward his, managing a smile. "And I won't look over my shoulder tonight. I promise."

The dinner was perfect and the music bright and happy. Several members of Daniel's church passed by, waved, and went on with their own fun. Daniel made no attempt to sit close to Carole, choosing rather to keep a discreet distance between them. But the festive atmosphere made her feel euphoric, and soon they were swept away on a tide of frivolity, trading one-liners and silly puns.

Like Cinderella, Carole was astonished to find the time so late, but she had no need to leave behind a glass slipper. She had an idea there would be other such occasions. Daniel Thornton was the perfect date.

She was whisked away to her door and she used the last few minutes of their time together to ask the traditional question.

"Would you like to come in for a cup of coffee?"

"Thanks, I'd like that."

She led him into the den, and as he settled into a deep-cushioned chair, she got out the cups and saucers. "Regular or Cappuccino?"

"Cappuccino, please. You have a lovely home."

She handed him the steaming cup. "Thank-you. I've thoroughly enjoyed owning a home of my own. It's wonderful to know that I can paint the bathroom purple if I want to, without worrying what the next pastor's wife's tastes might be."

"That is a problem, isn't it? I'm making arrangements right now with the congregation to buy the parsonage. It will be the first home I've ever owned. Congregations are beginning to change their policy about maintaining parsonages. It's really cheaper for them in the long run. Now I get to pay for the new water heater when it goes out." But his smile was a proud one.

"Are you happy in your new church?" asked Carole as she sat down across from him.

"Well, it really isn't that much different from my last place. People are people. This church seems to be a little more cosmopolitan than the last—more businessmen on executive levels. That's refreshing. Sometimes there is a larger gap to bridge when there are pronounced educational differences between the pastor and his flock."

"But I asked if you were happy," she repeated. "Or perhaps it's really none of my business."

"Yes . . . I'm happy." He looked thoughtful, contemplating her question. "I don't mind telling you it's lonely not having my wife to share the good and the bad times. Even my daughter Leigh is away most of the time at boarding school. But I'm basically happy. Coming to a new place is always a shot in the arm. The people are eager to get going again. Somehow I think they feel they are on hold when they have an interim pastor. But one of my greatest missions is to teach them that *they* are the church, not the *pastor.*'' His brown eyes opened wide as they looked into hers.

"Hmmm . . . I guess that's one of the primary goals of any good pastor."

"There are some strong lay people in this church, Carole, with a good concept of what it's all about. I'll be depending upon them to lead the way for the others." His glance at her was significant.

She fingered the lacy pattern on the side of her cup before continuing. "What do you like best about the ministry?"

"Working one-to-one with the people, I guess. Baptisms, weddings, communions, even funerals in a way, because I like being a part of their lives, even in sorrow."

"You're especially good at that," Carole smiled gratefully. "I remember when Samuel died I—I made it through largely because of your kindness." Her voice caught in her throat.

He shook his head. "Thanks, but let's be careful to keep in mind that ultimately it was your faith that pulled you through. I was only a temporary support system."

Regaining her composure, she replied lightly, "I guess that's why some women fall in love with their doctors or ministers."

"Don't laugh," he flinched. "It's an occupational hazard!"

She became very still. Words formed in her mind, but she chose them cautiously. "Daniel, I want to speak frankly about something." She faltered. "I want us to be friends, good friends. But I have the feeling you want more." He started to speak, so she went on quickly. "I'm afraid you're looking for more than I can give you. I really do like you.

Who could help but like such a charming, intelligent man? But I want you to be aware that I don't want any kind of serious relationship. I hope I'm not taking too much for granted, but we are spending a lot of time together, and I don't think bachelor pastors do that casually." She waited to see if she had made a complete fool of herself by speaking so soon. But he had to know that she had no intention of considering him anything more than a friend.

Weakly, he smiled. "You don't give a guy much room, do you?" She shook her head no. "Right now I just want to be your friend, Carole. I want to spend time with you because you're smart, attractive, and witty. But it's only fair to warn you that I am very attracted to you." He averted his eyes from hers, pausing for a long moment. "There is one thing I need to know, though. Is it all ministers you're avoiding, or just me?"

She turned to him, but he kept his eyes on his cup.

"I'm afraid of you, Daniel. You make me feel things again. You're someone I could care for, so I can't afford to get involved with you. God has chosen you to do special things. In my own way I do special things for Him, too, but I could never share the uniqueness of your life. You said I must have had some bitter times. The times weren't bitter, but some of the individual acts were. I found myself caught between the best people and the worst. I can't handle the worst ones any more. Most of the days were just average—cooking and cleaning and taking care of Samuel. But as I became caught up in more and more activities, I found myself doing things I didn't want to do just to avoid listening to the complaints that I wasn't like the last pastor's wife. The jobs I took because I really wanted to do them became drudges. But I couldn't get out of them gracefully."

"Without criticism, you mean?" He was watching her face now. His concentration was strong as she reached deep inside for an explanation—for him, for herself.

"I never thought of it that way."

"You know the saying that the way to avoid criticism is to do nothing? Would you actually keep yourself from loving someone just to avoid criticism? Even a bank president's wife or a farmer's wife might be criticized."

"I know, but I would expect that from the world."

He leaned toward her, forcing her to look deep into his eyes. "Don't shut me out, Carole. Things could be different this time. The only commitment I want from you right now is that you give us a chance to get to know each other. I won't hurt you." His earnestness constricted her throat and sent her pulse racing.

"I'm not afraid that *you'll* hurt me, Daniel. It's the people you serve. I do like you, Daniel. I'd like to be your friend, but that's all I can promise you for now."

"Good, that's all I could hope for—for now. Just don't shut me out of your life completely. Besides, you're the best punster I know," he added lightly. "I need to go. It's getting very late." He rose to leave.

As they reached the door, she said, "I had a special time tonight. Thank-you for asking me out." She had really expected a light kiss on the forehead, or maybe the cheek. She wasn't quite prepared for his friendly handshake. But there he was, shaking her hand and telling her what a pleasant evening it had been. He left with promises of doing this again soon. She was already walking down the hallway before she realized she was disappointed that he hadn't at least tried to kiss her good night. He was making it easy for her to keep her resolve not to get involved with another man of the cloth—or was he?

## CHAPTER 3

CAROLE LOVED LAZY Saturday mornings. Still in her night-gown, she took her coffee out into the garden. The air was humid, coaxing the white flowers of the magnolia tree to give off all their lemony fragrance. Each waxy petal was limp with the effort.

She stretched out languidly in the lounger and pulled the gown up higher on her legs to let the sun play on them. Getting a gentle start on her day, Carole made a mental list of things she needed to do. *Pick up cleaning.* She yawned. *Call Joyce about the tea next week.* She sipped lovingly at the aromatic coffee. *And I need to decide whether or not to go to the church picnic,* she concluded, satisfied that she had an agenda. The phone interrupted her planning.

"Hi, Carole, this is Joyce. Are you busy?"

*Are you busy?* was her best friend's euphemism for *Can you talk a long time?*

"No. In fact, I have you on my list of people to call today." Carole settled onto the gray chaise lounge.

"How far down the list am I?"

"Right on top now. What can I do for you?"

"Are you going to the church picnic today?"

"Sure. Want to go together?"

"I'll come get you about one. Don't bring any food, though. This is a fund-raiser for the Ladies Guild. Just bring a lot of lettuce." Joyce chortled at her own joke.

"Oh, Joyce, that's terrible," Carole groaned. "You're a bad influence on me. Maybe I ought to reconsider."

"Be ready," she threatened, "or I'll tell Teletype Tillie that you're dating Daniel. Bye."

"Wait, Joyce, how did you know?" But Joyce was already gone.

Carole dressed casually in a pair of kelly green slacks topped with a floral print cotton blouse, put out her favorite yellow tennis shoes, and added a swimsuit. *Beach towel,* she reminded herself. She pulled her heavy hair back with a perky green ribbon. Because of the heat, she used little makeup, but she lavishly sprayed on her favorite perfume. It was a light fragrance of which she never tired.

A little after one she heard the horn of Joyce's red sports car. Grabbing her shoes and the small beach bag, she ran barefoot to the car.

"My gosh, Carole, you look fantastic," complained Joyce. "How do you do it?" she asked glumly.

"I'm glad to see you, too, Happy," and she made a sorrowful face. "Love your Levis."

"I love them, too, and it's a good thing. For what I paid, I'll have to wear them every day for the rest of my unnatural life to break even." Joyce smiled as she watched Carole slip on her shoes and tie them. "Grown-up time, huh?"

Carole grinned at the reference to her habit of wearing shoes only when forced.

The drive to Lake o' Pines went beyond beautiful for

Carole. Even the oppressive humidity couldn't wilt the majesty of the long-needled pines or the stateliness of the ruffled leafed oaks. Carole loved this land fiercely. She remembered the first day she had driven into Longview and the curious feeling of familiarity she had experienced. She had remarked laughingly to friends, "If I believed in reincarnation, I'd swear I'd lived here before." She seemed to know where to turn before she knew the names of the streets. In a way she had truly grown up here, and she had no intentions of ever leaving her real home. Her eyes drank in the lushness around her. There were no painful memories here in her green heaven. She smiled serenely to herself as parts of the Book of Ecclesiastes drifted back to her.

*For everything there is a season and a time for every matter under heaven:*
*. . . a time to mourn and a time to dance;*
*a time to cast away stones, and a time to gather stones together . . .*

". . . air conditioning," said Joyce.

"What?" At the sound of Joyce's words Carole forced her attention back to the present.

"I said, let's turn off the air conditioning and roll down the windows. Might as well enjoy the smell as well as the view." Soon the wind was buffeting them with a sweet pine-scented breeze.

"Did you bring a swimsuit?" asked Joyce. She looked pretty with the wind tousling her short black hair.

"Right here in my little bag. How about you?"

"Yup. Right here in my *big* bag." Joyce was famous for her large tote bag in which she seemed to have any needed item at any given moment.

"Is it true that in case of nuclear attack you could survive out of that bag for a month?" Carole's eyes were wide with innocence.

35

"Nope. Only three weeks." Joyce smiled good-naturedly. "Incidentally, how was your date?" she countered.

"How did you know about that?"

"Do you think you can go to a public place and not be noticed?" she replied. "Tillie picked it up on her line, and now the entire world knows. Well, don't keep me in suspense. What happened?" demanded Joyce.

"I had a lovely time. We went to that new place that just opened and we had dinner and talked the night away," Carole summarized briefly. "It's been a long time since I've had such a pleasant evening."

"Sounds to me like you went out with a business acquaintance," commented Joyce dryly. "Wasn't it romantic or anything? I mean did he . . . no, never mind, I don't really want to know. I am just trying to imagine what going out with your pastor must be like. If you want to know the truth, it sort of boggles my mind."

"For heaven's sake, Joyce, he's just a man. I mean, he's not *just* a man, but he isn't a stuffed shirt or a plaster saint."

"What do you say to a pastor on a date?" she asked, puzzlement clearly marking her brow.

"Well, first of all he gave me a preview of next week's sermon, and then we discussed homiletics. Really, Joyce, why are you making this so hard for me?"

"Hard for you? I've never dated a minister before. I've never even spent time with a Sunday school teacher, except for a woman teacher. And that hardly counts."

"Look, old friend, he just happens to have a weekend job. Oh, Joyce, you know better than to stereotype people. He's a man, we went out together, and we had a good time. Just let it go at that." Joyce was beginning to sound a lot like too many other people she had known, and maybe a little too much like Carole herself. She chuckled. "No, he didn't kiss me good night."

"Well, that's what I wanted to know in the first place. I won't tell a soul. Besides, what would I have to tell?" Joyce's eyes gleamed with mirth. "The next, and most important question: Will you go out with him again?"

"Maybe a better question is, Will he ask me out again?" She added rather casually. "Joyce, do you know if he is going with anyone, seriously I mean?"

"If he is, it's a deep dark secret." Joyce's careless tone was suddenly tinged with suspicion. Her eyes narrowed. "Why? Are you interested?"

"Oh, heavens, no," was the flippant reply.

"But you have gone out with him—and you would again—" pressed Joyce.

"Maybe," replied Carole guardedly. "Look, Joyce," she said firmly, "I'm not getting trapped in that life again. I just wondered, that's all."

Looking out the window was a good way to avoid direct eye contact with Joyce. She wasn't sure what Joyce might read in her eyes.

Lake o' Pines lay sparkling blue under a brilliant sky. The boats looked like toys; and the skiers they pulled, like miniature puppets that were suddenly jerked on invisible strings when they toppeled into the water.

Just before reaching the dam, Joyce turned the car off to the left and descended to the sandy beached swimming and boating area. It was exceptionally crowded, and she had to park a good distance away.

There were fires going in most of the small fireplaces, and food was piled high on concrete picnic tables decorated with colorful red-checked cloths. Boats made regular stops at the boat docks to take on new passengers and skiers. Looking like a flock of multicolored birds, children splashed in the roped-off swim area. Sitting comfortably in the shade of the enormous pines were adults designated as temporary lifeguards. Ice cream makers were packed in towels to keep the salted ice from melting. And tempting cakes, waiting to be cut, were displayed on a deeply shaded picnic table.

"Here," Joyce said enthusiastically, "have a paper plate and dig in."

"Have you ever noticed how much better food tastes when you eat it outside?" purred Carole, passing up the steaming red pinto beans for a snowy mound of potato salad.

"I know our Ladies Guild makes the best barbequed ribs in Texas," replied Joyce. She licked the smokey-tasting sauce off her finger to add proof to her claim.

The two women sat at a table under the towering pine trees and savored both the food and a panoramic view of the glittering lake. It was all so perfect, and they knew it was about to end as they saw Teletype Tillie bearing down on them like a hunting dog on the scent of quail.

"Oh, no," groaned Joyce and Carole simultaneously, but neither of them moved, mesmerized as much by Tillie's determined movements as by their good manners.

Her thin body, clad in a red denim sun dress, was topped by an angular face. As she made her way toward them, Carole noticed her immaculate white orthopedic shoes and a matching straw hat. The hat didn't hide the flaming red hair, kept carefully dyed the color of yesteryear. Her heavily rouged cheeks crinkled in a big smile as she juggled a plate of food and a glass of iced tea, and then registered annoyance as some of the tea splashed out of the glass to soil her new shoes.

As Tillie neared her targets, Carole mused that all those years of tracking down the latest gossip had honed her to mere bones. Her own welcoming smile was weak and unconvincing. *Shame on you, Carole Morgan,* she admonished herself. *Where is your Christian charity?* But she noticed that Joyce was taking a large bite of food that excused her from answering Tillie's opening question.

"Mind if I sit here, girls?" Without waiting for an affirmative answer, she zeroed in for a landing like a duck on a June bug. She sat facing Carole, her back to the lake.

"I'd rather sit where I can't see those brazen teenage girls bouncing around in those skimpy swimsuits. No wonder so many of them are gettin' into trouble. Loretta Gray ought to hide her head in shame, lettin' her only daughter run around like that." She fairly bristled with indignation, but her insatiable curiosity made her turn to Carole and Joyce for the news. "And how are things with you girls?"

Neither Carole nor Joyce wanted to chance becoming fodder for her verbal cannons, so they replied with cautious non-news.

Disconcerted that she had learned nothing, Tillie tacked into the wind and asked point-blank, "How was your date with Pastor?" The brim of her straw hat quivered like an antenna waiting to receive a message.

But Carole was an expert in avoiding this type of woman and her embellished retellings of conversations, so she used a question to answer a question. "How did you know about that?"

"Oh, honey, everybody's talking about it. Anything serious between you two?" Her long thin nose twitched in anticipation.

"If so, you'll be the first to know," smiled Carole truthfully.

Joyce seemed to be having trouble swallowing a large bite of macaroni salad. "Too much dill pickle juice, I guess," Joyce choked.

"Are you all right, dear?" Tillie asked, her eyes roaming the crowds at the edge of the pine trees. Without waiting for an answer, she exclaimed, "There's Pastor Thornton now! I wondered where he'd gone off to. He *is* a handsome devil, isn't he? Kind of reminds me of my late husband, Harold, in his prime—God rest his soul. I wonder how come he's never remarried. Sure has had lots of chances. Dozens of women I know would have jumped at the chance.

"I hear that nice Mrs. Willingham has the inside track now. He took her to dinner a couple of weeks ago. Such a pretty thing she is, too," and she leaned forward as she warmed to her subject.

Carole didn't want to hear Daniel's name coming from this woman's parrot-like mouth, but she was interested in the information in spite of herself. She asked no questions to spur Tillie on, but then Tillie needed none.

"Then he took her to the symphony," she continued. "He'd need a classy lady for a wife, his being a minister and all. She's classy all right. Dresses real nice," she offered. "Pays a pretty penny for those clothes, I'll bet. I hear she inherited a lot of money from her father. He was a judge, you know."

Joyce was sitting stock-still, her mouth gaping open.

*How lonely Tillie must be,* Carole thought sympathetically. Tillie's tongue was not malicious. Her assaults were mostly the wishful living of other people's lives. Still, her news caused a sinking sensation in the pit of Carole's stomach and, suddenly unable to eat another bite, she stood and reached for her plate. Following suit, Joyce snapped out of her trance and quickly gathered up her debris.

"It was nice talking to you, Tillie," Carole said politely, and turning to Joyce, she asked, "Ready for a swim?"

"You girls shouldn't go in the water so soon after eating," Tillie intoned in a motherly way.

"Well, maybe we'll just boat awhile first," Joyce replied quickly lest the loss of the excuse keep them at the table for more verbal batterings.

"Better be careful about that, too," said Tillie ominously. "There's a summer storm brewing. I've seen 'em before. Come up real sudden-like out of the north, blowing cold and mean." Her eyebrows were pulled together vertically, emphasizing her words.

Both women automatically checked the hot, cloudless blue sky doubtfully. Seeing their disbelief, Tillie repeated her warning, adding mysteriously, "It's August."

"Then we'll need to hurry before it gets here," Joyce said in a determined voice. "Bye, Tillie," and she grabbed Carole's arm, moving her quickly away.

They hurried to the brick dressing rooms to change, laughing at Tillie's dire predictions. Joyce came out of the cubicles last, looking down in exasperation. "I guess I should have passed up the cake and ice cream. I look like a baby whale."

Carole's laugh was gentle as she eyed her friend's slightly pudgy figure. "Oh, Joyce, you look fine," she protested lovingly.

"Sure I do. Honestly, Carole, sometimes God is so unfair. You look smashing in that swimsuit."

Carole *was* pleased that her black one-piece suit molded her slender figure, accentuating her curves, yet maintained her modesty. And with her shimmering hair piled high, Joyce declared that she looked as regal as a princess.

Eyeing Carole's tiny waist, her friend blurted thoughtlessly, "Maybe it's because you never had kids."

Seeing the sudden pain flood Carole's eyes, Joyce grabbed her arm and pleaded, "Oh, Carole, I'm sorry! I could bite off my tongue!" Tears welled up in her own dark eyes, but Carole patted her hand. "It's all right, Joyce," and in an overly bright voice, she finished the conversation. "Let's hit the water, kid. We don't have much time before the storm hits. It's August, you know."

They hurried to the docks just in case Tillie was watching, and clambered into the first available boat.

"Room for one more!" shouted Phillip, who was happily ferrying the picnickers in his new boat. "Hey, Pastor, come on! There's room for one more." Carole's heart constricted her chest.

As he climbed aboard, Daniel laughed, "Just Daniel, Phil. I'm here socially, not in my official capacity," and he plopped down into the seat next to Carole. "Hello, there. Mind if I sit next to you?" he asked her, friendly as a puppy.

"Guess not, since it's the last seat," she said a little more curtly than she intended.

He looked at her in mild surprise, noting the shortness of her answer. He tried again. "Having a good time today? You look terrific in that suit." There was genuine appreciation in his compliment.

Matching his attempt at casual conversation, she smiled and said, "Yes, and thank-you." Carole made a determined effort to halt the surge of pleasure she felt at seeing him again and looked across the lake, averting her eyes from the unsettling effect of his tanned, strong body clad in swim trunks and an open shirt.

The roar of the motor made it difficult to talk, which suited Carole just fine. As the boat cut through the clear lake water, it threw a fine spray on her warm skin. Soon she was lightly jeweled with tiny droplets, and her skin grew warmer as she felt Daniel's eyes on her.

He leaned closer to her to shout something in her ear. She could smell that familiar scent he used, and she desperately wished she didn't have to move so closely to him to answer.

His dark eyes twinkled as she leaned toward him, modestly covering the front of her suit with her hand to shield the swell of her breast. She blushed as she realized what she had done, but stubbornly refused to move that hand. Mumbling something inane, she rapidly leaned back into the shelter of her seat. *Some minister he is,* she muttered safely under her breath. But in her marriage she had found her man of the cloth to be very passionate. And she knew most ministers seemed to enjoy all of God's gifts to the fullest—a fact they generally hid from their congregations, lest they be criticized for being too worldly. In the eyes of some, holiness and passion were incompatible.

Phillip expertly navigated the boat into the dock at Bass Cove, and Carole poked Joyce, signaling that they were to get out. Without a backward glance, she led the way up to the bait house, where fishing supplies were sold. She quickly bought two soft drinks and abruptly herded Joyce out a side door.

Joyce turned around, her hands on her hips. "Hey, what's wrong with you?"

"I'm mad! Can't you tell?"

"What did I do?" demanded Joyce.

"It's not you. I'm sorry I snapped." She stole a glance around the area, searching for the target of her anger. "I just don't like the way *some* people act." Her eyes riveted Daniel's unsuspecting back. "Joyce, I think I'd like to have a little time for myself. I'll walk to the next cove and catch the boat there. Okay?"

"Sure." Joyce's eyes were forgiving. "A walk in the woods will give you time to cool off. What did he say to you?"

"It wasn't *what* he said, it was the *way* he said it. See you in a little while." She scurried off, eager to escape her own conflicting emotions.

Walking under an umbrella of huge pine boughs was soothing. The easy trail was worn down from the footprints

43

of many hikers. She could hear a mockingbird staking out his territory with his song and another answering with a chirp. The air was quite humid, and the smell of the damp forest and lake water created an earthy perfume. Tall, thick trees limited her view of the sky, but she could hear the boats and squeals of laughter from the water-skiers as they raced across the lake.

She felt calm now, and more than a little foolish. But she had started this charade and she would have to see it through. At least this was a pleasant way of walking off her chagrin.

As she rounded a curve in the path, she noticed the air had developed a sudden chill bite. She glanced up. The small patches of sky that shortly before had been blue were now shrouded in dark, boiling clouds. Tillie had been right. A storm was brewing.

The ominously smooth, steady roll of thunder began, followed by a jerky crackling one, but there was no visible lightning. As the wind picked up, the temperature began to fall rapidly.

Carole felt the edges of panic nudging her. Shelter was the single thought in her mind. She was closer to the Cove than to the bait house, and since she couldn't stay here she'd better get moving. Once committed to a plan of action, she felt better.

The cold drops of rain began to fall, splattering the dust of the path as they hit. Carole was jogging, breathing evenly and watching carefully for snags in the unfamiliar path. The drops became huge and soon they were pelting down on her with alarming force. Even the thick branches of the trees provided little protection.

The wind moaning through the trees unnerved her and she stumbled along the path, blinded by sheets of cold, drenching rain. Her breathing was ragged from fear and exertion.

She was running with her head down, trying to make out the path, when she crashed into something solid. Through rain-soaked hair and eyes, she saw it was Daniel. He grabbed her hand and led her off the path through bushes that tugged and pulled, as if to tear them apart.

Suddenly, right in front of them, was a small shed hidden by brush and rain. Daniel pulled her into the dark interior and shut the door against the angry storm.

She couldn't see a thing, but still holding on to Daniel's hand, she followed him into the room. It felt heavenly after the cold wind and rain. As her eyes adjusted to the dark, she could see a tiny window, the light barely penetrating the heavy grime.

Daniel fumbled around for something for them to sit on. Finding a wooden bench in a darkened corner, he dragged it out into the middle of the room.

"Here you are, milady," he said gallantly, and she sank down gratefully on the rough planks.

"How did you find me?" she began, and realizing that sounded like a line out of an old movie, began again. "Boy, am I glad to see you!" It wasn't much better.

"May I place my soggy self beside you, this being the last seat?" he asked, grinning mischievously.

"I blush that you should ask me sir," she grinned back.

"I wish I had something to offer in the way of warm clothing. I know you're cold in that wet swimsuit."

Squinting into the darkness, Carole said triumphantly, "Hey! There's a small stove or something."

Upon closer investigation it turned out to be a "something." But they did find an old army blanket on the shelf. After a careful shaking, Daniel dropped it over her shivering body, then searched in vain for another one. She dreaded sitting close to him, but courtesy alone demanded that she offer part of the blanket.

"Come on—I'll share." Her offer was grudgingly made.

"How can I refuse such a warm and generous offer?" he joked.

It took some juggling and rearranging for both of them to gain maximum coverage, but at least they were warmer. Carole was surprised to find that she didn't feel at all uncomfortable beside him. In fact, it felt rather nice.

"You know, there's a Bible verse that talks about keeping each other warm," he remarked.

"What Bible verse?" she challenged.

"'And if your brother has only one cloak, share it with him,'" he quoted solemnly. She laughed aloud. "You made that up!"

"Well, maybe it is a loose translation," he admitted, chuckling.

The small talk tapered off and they sat in silence for a few minutes listening to the raging storm.

"Hope everyone got off the lake," she worried.

"I'm sure they did. Most of us realized what was happening in time."

"Are you going to tell me how you found me?"

"I saw you leave the bait house by the side door. There was only one path you could have taken. I knew you couldn't see the storm coming, so I got off at Fisherman's Cove and started walking back. I remembered this old camping shack from my trip out here last week, and figured we could make it."

She shivered as she remembered her fear on the path out there in the blinding rain.

"Still cold? Here, cuddle up closer to me. I won't bite," he said kindly.

If she hadn't been so cold and miserable, she would have refused. As it was, she had little choice. It occurred to her that they might both be more comfortable if they sat on the floor and used the bench for a back rest.

"Good idea," he applauded. "Here, let me move the bench like this. Now, that should be better."

It was much better, and she really didn't mind being nestled cozily beside him. But she blocked out the details of what made it so much better.

"You even look pretty with your hair wet," he murmured softly, and touched a damp curl near her face with gentle fingers. The corners of her mouth curved upward.

The pale light silhouetted his face. His dark hair had curled with the rain, accentuating the strength of his jawline. In profile, his nose was reminiscent of the Greek statues, long and straight. Time had served him well, she thought, filling the deep-set brown eyes with compassion and verve. And then the nearness of him came to her quite clearly. His bare shoulder resting against hers, his brown leg propped up for support. It didn't seem at all odd when his arm moved up and around her. And even more natural to turn her face to him and raise her soft lips for his kiss.

It was a gentle, searching kiss. The man's mouth was new to her, but the feelings it evoked were much too familiar. Carole felt herself sliding into the past, responding to her body's memory of Samuel's mouth—not Daniel's—and a raw need began to melt her will as he tightened his arms around her. It was Daniel's kiss, but her heart was blind in her urgent need to have this feeling go on and on.

To her anguish, he wrenched away from her, his trembling hands resting on her shoulders as he looked deeply into her eyes.

"I'm sorry, Carole, I didn't mean to take advantage of the situation."

Her dismay was unbounded, but she couldn't speak. He got unsteadily to his feet and pulled her up in one easy motion. Moving away from her with averted eyes, he said in a dark voice, "Don't worry. I know how you feel about involvement with a minister. It won't happen again." Relief crept into his voice as he looked out the window. "I think the storm is letting up. We'd better go."

But the storm within Carole's heart had just begun. From the warmth of a summer day, her emotions were now buffeted by the cold wind of rejection.

Dumbly she pulled the blanket around her shivering shoulders and tried to control her shaky legs. *What is the matter with me?* Her cheeks flamed as she remembered the physical feelings that had suddenly broken to the surface. Did Daniel realize how intense a response he had jolted from her with his kiss? She prayed he had not. How would she ever face him again? Knowing that the need was strictly physical did nothing to ease her embarrassment.

Following him through the light drizzle that was still misting the path gave her time to recover her composure, but not to sort out the conflicting emotions swirling in her mind. By the time they finally got to Fisherman's Cove, Carole knew only one fact for sure—she had to stay away from Daniel. He awakened feelings she thought had been buried five years ago. Never again would she take the chance that he might destroy her carefully constructed defenses. *Never,* she vowed to herself as they plodded along silently under the dripping trees.

They heard Phillip shouting their names as they neared the dock. His relief at finding them was enthusiastic, and if he saw anything unusual in finding them together, it was not evident. "Daniel! Carole! I just knew you'd be all right," he whooped. "I just knew it! Soaked to the skin, are you? Here, give me that soggy blanket, Carole, and take this dry slicker. Here's one for you, too, Daniel. And there's hot coffee in the thermos." He got them settled in the boat and headed back across the lake.

Phillip never asked where they had been during the storm. It would have been against his nature to assume the worst about anyone, Carole realized with surprise. He was genuinely glad to see them. They were safe, and that was all that mattered.

Daniel leaned close to Phillip and shouted, "That really was a bad one. Everybody all right?" At Phil's nod, Daniel sighed deeply and sank back into his seat. There was only the sound of the boat slapping through the choppy waves for the rest of the ride.

The rain was almost over, though the storm clouds could still be seen sliding off southward. Trying to get in a few last rays before setting, the sun had turned the sky an ethereal gold. Splashing the sky with soft artist's colors, a huge rainbow again proclaimed the Old Testament promise.

Daniel smiled a little wearily and said, "I feel a bit like old Noah."

Summoning the last of her reserves, Carole met his weak smile and replied, "The promise was, it would never happen again."

His eyes told her that he understood perfectly.

Carole was thankful that only Joyce and Phillip's wife Bernice were waiting for them. They jumped out of the shelter of Joyce's car to greet them.

"Thank God, you're safe!" exclaimed Bernice. With the assurance that all was well, they left to go their separate ways.

Carole crawled into Joyce's car and tried to think of a way to answer the questions that were sure to come. She was too tired to think quickly, so she went on the offensive. "Where were *you* when the storm hit?" she asked Joyce.

"We were already back on this side of the lake. Oh, Carole, I was so worried about you. If it hadn't been for that silly tiff . . ." She saw that there was no need for them to discuss what had happened. "As soon as it was safe, Phillip and the others started looking for everybody on this side of the lake. Most were scattered along in the coves, waiting in the bait houses."

"Right. That's where they picked us up."

It wasn't exactly a lie. But she didn't want even Joyce to know that she and Daniel had spent the storm in the deserted shack—alone. All the way home she kept up a steady stream of light conversation. And Joyce was too sensitive to interrogate her friend further.

Carole let herself into the house by the side door and went straight to the comfort of a warm bath. She sank into the fragrant bubbles up to her chin, closed her eyes, and willed herself not to think. What had happened, had happened. But it had changed things forever. Daniel's mouth was forever imprinted on her own and the memory of his arms wrapped around her made his rejection a bitter postlude to the memorable day. *I didn't want this to happen,* she thought hotly, and then she felt the tears rushing down her cheeks. For years she hadn't cried over a man, nor had her entire body responded so eagerly to a simple kiss.

As the tears washed the pain from her heart, a new thought struck her so forcibly that she sat straight up in the square tub. He *had* wanted her, really wanted her. She was quite sure of that. Surely he was not the type of man to kiss a woman with such ardor if he did not care for her. Then her eyes narrowed with another thought. Maybe there was more to Tillie's story about Mrs. Willingham than had been told. But there was one thing Carole knew instinctively. Something was growing between them. The real question was, Did she want him?

That, of course, was the dilemma.

It was very, very late when she slipped into her pale green

nightgown. She unpinned her silky hair and slid between the cool sheets. The day had taken its toll, and she didn't even finish her nightly prayers before she was journeying through the stars.

## CHAPTER 4

CAROLE'S EYES FLUTTERED open unwillingly in the half-light of her bedroom. Was it time to get up? What day was it? She reached for the alarm on the clock radio and, in the haze of her interrupted slumber, she remembered it was Sunday morning. Hair tumbling down around her sleep-softened face, she slipped into the matching peignoir of her gown, and pulling the soft green ribbon loosely around her waist to secure it, walked into the kitchen.

Last night's events began floating into her consciousness, and with them came Daniel's presence. She could easily imagine his Sunday morning routine. After all, that had been part of her life for a long time, too.

Sunday had been the high point of the week when she had been married to Samuel. Gentle excitement permeated the house as the shower ran, the bacon cooked, and Sunday clothes were donned for the worship service. Just before she left the house for her adult Bible class, she usually slipped a roast in the oven for lunch. When they returned, they were met by the mouth-watering aroma of their Sunday meal.

The worship services were treasures to her. The full church, her friends gathered for that one hour to hear God speak to them through their pastor, the hymns that sometimes brought tears of joy to her eyes, the prayers prayed in petition to the Lord for His intervention in their lives, the thank-you prayers for his many blessings—all these age-old acts of worship gave her a sense of peace and strength to carry her through another week, until the cycle was renewed.

And now it was time for that high point again, and she felt herself falling into the pattern so well known to her. The only difference was that now everything was colored by Daniel's presence, and her chaotic feelings for him.

Sparkling skies bathed the morning as she wound her way up the hill to the church. The scene reminded Carole of the Scripture verses about Jerusalem the Golden, for the white brick building shining in the sunlight resembled "a city set on a hillside."

Everything looked the same inside, but Carole knew as she scanned the faces of the congregation that things would never be quite the same again. She was uncomfortable with her new feelings. Was it only her imagination that Teletype Tillie smiled knowingly at her? Her cheeks warmed slightly, and she dropped her eyes to the well-loved words printed on the hymnal.

Daniel entered from his study door and stood by his ornate wooden chair. He sang heartily and, as his eyes passed briefly across Carole's, she realized with a start that there was not a flicker of recognition in them. *He means to keep his promise,* she thought. *He will never touch me again.* She felt a stab of disappointment that she would not have to make any choices. Obviously, he had chosen for both of them.

She moved automatically with the flow of the service,

53

standing and sitting at the proper times. She successfully blocked out the sound of Daniel's voice until all she heard was a muffled sound mingling with the hum of the air conditioner. So she would go home with her cup empty this week. During the sermon she stared at the wall just behind his head to avoid his handsome face, so intent on the delivery of his sermon.

But afterward there was no way she could avoid being ushered down the aisle and marched past him for a friendly greeting at the church door. *O Lord,* she prayed silently, *be merciful to me, and make me disappear like Elijah in the fiery chariot.* But she felt more like Lot's wife, a pillar of salt, with feet moving her closer and closer to the source of Daniel's cheerful voice.

"Good morning, Carole," he said in a perfectly natural tone. "Glad to see you're no worse for wear from that storm yesterday. It was really something, wasn't it?"

Her hand in his was numb; her smile, automatic; her tongue, dumb. She nodded in what she desperately hoped was a casual way, but felt her head move woodenly—like a marionette's. Her leaden feet took her past him and out the door.

As she stepped into the blinding sunlight, a bony arm shot out and matching fingers clutched her arm, pulling her around to meet the piercingly inquisitive eyes of Teletype Tillie.

"Carole, I'm so glad I bumped into you. About yesterday . . . I was just wonderin' . . ." Suddenly Tillie's voice rose to a high-pitched shriek, descending to a shuddering gasp as Joyce lurched into her, splashing water out of the flower vase she was carrying.

"Tillie! Oh, I'm so sorry! I couldn't see where I was going over all these altar flowers. Here, let me help you." She juggled the floral arrangement, dabbing at the back of

Tillie's purple shirtwaist dress. But her efforts seemed to be doing more harm than good, and the flowers she held were now swishing back and forth in Tillie's face. "Here, hold these, Tillie," said Joyce, shoving the blossoms under her beak-like nose.

"Stop!" she squawked. "Stop! Let me do it myself!"

"Well, all right, Tillie," Joyce agreed reluctantly. "I'm really sorry. At least, let me try to mop up some of that water."

"No, never mind." Tillie turned and harumphed away.

"Hey, Tillie, I hope this won't affect our friendship," shouted the penitent Joyce after her, the words bouncing off Tillie's angry, wet back.

Carole turned grateful eyes to Joyce. "You're certainly getting careless in your old age—thank goodness."

"Well, water is good for putting out small fires before they get out of hand."

"How about a glass of cool mint tea this afternoon around four o'clock?"

"Sounds good to me. Uh-oh, now might be a good time for you to disappear into the sunset. I think I just saw a flash of purple." Joyce's eyes twinkled. "I doubt that I could get by with that stunt twice in one day."

"You're a jewel. See you later." And Carole walked away from the church briskly as Joyce intercepted Tillie with great concern for her water-soaked dress.

Carole was still smiling as she climbed into her car, but the smile wilted as she recalled the reason for Tillie's curiosity. Daniel had, indeed, provided an excellent performance for the people around them, she thought indignantly. How could he act so normally when she was still shaken from the intensity of their encounter? How could he touch her hand without a trace of emotion? Her growing anger caused her to accelerate the little car, and it responded by leaping past the other plodding cars. Speeding down the road, however, did nothing to soothe her and, catching sight of a patrol car ahead, she automatically slowed her speed.

*I've never felt so humiliated,* she fumed. *I really thought he was feeling something for me. But it wasn't me.* With the bitter discovery came tears. *Any woman could have brought out that response in him,* she reasoned. *I just happened to be available. It didn't mean a thing.* A long sigh escaped her parted lips. Her defenses were breached and, against all her own advice, she knew she was falling in love with Rev. Daniel Thornton.

But the argument resumed. *I could never, never marry another minister and walk willingly into a lifestyle I left behind. No love,* she thought, *could ever be worth the heartache. He has made it plain he doesn't intend to pursue the matter, so I should be grateful to him for making it so easy. I can just let it go—like that,* and she snapped her fingers to seal the bargain with herself. At that point Carole realized she was blocks past the turn to her house.

At the sound of the doorbell, Carole's spirits lifted. *A good visit with Joyce is just what I need.* She smiled and opened the door. "Hi, come on in. I think you might be just in time for high tea."

"What's that heavenly aroma wafting from your kitchen?"

"Oh, that. It's just some of those tiny little pecan pies. Don't worry, I won't offer you any. I know how careful you are about your figure. I'm baking these for a little gray-haired grandmother I know."

Joyce immediately assumed a bent-backed stance and pantomimed walking with a cane. "Well, now, daughter, that was right friendly of you to think of an old lady," she said in a high-pitched, quavering voice. Once she was in the kitchen, she offered solicitously, "Here, let me take that heavy tray of goodies out to the patio for you. You carry the lighter tea tray."

"Your thoughtfulness is exceeded only by your greed," Carole grinned. "Thank-you so much. Do you think you could open the door for me, too?"

Joyce expertly maneuvered her elbow between the handle of the sliding door and the doorjamb. "Allow me, madam," and she stepped aside, bowing slightly.

They placed the trays on the glass-topped table and sat down in the cool shade of the heavy-leafed magnolia tree. Carole opened the little sugar bowl. "Three lumps?"

"Goodness, no, only two since I'm having several of those tiny little treats."

"I like a woman who knows how to take care of herself."

"Speaking of taking care of oneself, I noticed you seem to have a bit of blue under your eyes. Or is that a new way to wear eye shadow?" It was not an unkind remark.

"The only thing I seem to know right now is that I am balancing precariously on the edge of making a fool of myself." Looking Joyce squarely in the eye, she confessed, "I've never pretended to you that my marriage to Samuel was perfect. Most people think that if you live in a parsonage, nothing bad ever happens to you. You never disagree. There are no tough decisions to make. You are immune to pain of any kind. Samuel used to tell people that there's no such thing as a 'parsonage passover,' and that the Devil works even harder to mess up Christians." She sipped her tea thoughtfully. "I loved my husband very much. The thing that made me the most unhappy was not the minor disagreements I had with Samuel, but the way some people in our congregation tried to run our lives.

"When we first married, I played the role of pastor's wife to the hilt." Her gaze wandered to the top of the tree, focusing on yesterdays. "I really did my best to make everyone happy. And most of the people in our churches were really good people. But there was always someone who knew just what I was supposed to be doing."

Her brow puckered vertically with remembered humiliation. "I never learned to deal with it. I did all the things I thought a pastor's wife was expected to do. I took every job that needed doing when no one else would do it."

Helplessly she shook her head. "But I knew I was spreading myself too thin. I honestly didn't know how to get out . . . and it broke my heart when they complained to me about Samuel.

Her eyes glistened with unshed tears. "I held Samuel in my arms as he broke down and cried over a particularly vicious letter. Remembering that, it's hard to recall the kindness—the home-baked bread, the generous gifts, the floods of love and good wishes. I can't reconcile what Samuel preached with the way some Christians treat each other."

There was a long pause after Carole's outburst. The two women sat in silence, pondering the things she had said until Joyce ventured softly, "You mean you really haven't forgiven all those people who hurt you and Samuel and each other. Isn't that really what you're saying?" Joyce was watching her carefully.

Carole winced. "Of course, I've forgiven them!"

Joyce did not pursue her statement. "I can see why you have a few blue shadows under your eyes. What are you going to do about Daniel?"

"Run like mad! I just couldn't go through all that again."

Her succinct answer didn't surprise Joyce. A tear slid down Carole's soft cheek. "You're the best. Thanks for listening."

Any time. Only next time we have a heart-to-heart talk,

please don't bake little pecan pies. I'm on my fourth." Carole's silvery laugh dried the last vestige of tears. She felt a new resolve to stay away from Daniel, and with it a serenity that had been missing of late.

Carole's new outlook on life was put to the test a few evenings later when Daniel called her at home. Surprisingly her heart didn't leap into her throat when she heard his voice speaking her name.

"Hello, Carole."

"Hello, Daniel." She felt no need to make small talk. He had called her. Let him do the talking. She felt a little proud of herself. No more silly schoolgirl nonsense.

"I felt that I should call you and do a little explaining." He was the one who sounded uncomfortable.

"About what?"

"I'm still feeling guilty about what happened at the lake. I just wanted to be sure you weren't mad at me." He did sound worried.

"I'm not mad at you, Daniel. It was just something that happened under unusual circumstances. I know you weren't trying to take advantage of me. It's over and forgotten." The finality in her voice was apparent.

"Would you let me take you to dinner to atone?"

"There's really nothing to atone for, and if there were, a dinner certainly wouldn't cover it."

"What would?"

"Oh, a mink coat or a diamond bracelet." Her words were carefully indifferent.

"Your atonements are certainly expensive!" he laughed. "Would you settle for a movie?"

"If I say no, are you going to counteroffer with a trip to the ice cream parlor?"

"Probably. Pastors usually find a tactful way of getting

what they want. I'll up the ante to the Bensons' Labor Day party. How about letting me off the hook?''

"Not a chance. I think I like having the upper hand. Besides, I've already made plans for that party.''

"Well, you'll be sorry. I'm terrific at Labor Day parties.''

"I guess I'll just have to take the chance of having a dull time. Thanks for asking, though. Maybe some other time.''

"I'll hold you to that promise,'' he replied good-naturedly. "Good-by now.''

"Good-by, Daniel.'' She hung up the phone with a definite sense of accomplishment.

The Bensons' Labor Day party always kicked off the fall season. Everybody would be there. It was the annual event that people talked about for weeks. James and Betty Benson's lake house was the perfect setting for enormous gatherings, for there was boating, water skiing, tennis, swimming in the lake or the Olympic-sized pool, horseshoes, and even horseback riding. At dusk, the sides of barbequed beef that had been roasting on open spits would be sliced and placed on the groaning buffet table under a canopy of ancient water oaks and hackberry trees.

Carole attended the party without an escort. She was comfortable meeting her friends there and moving from group to group. Her white eyelet sundress set off her bronzed shoulders and, on the practical side, she had pulled back her dark auburn hair in a cool and casual style and secured it with two red combs that matched her low-heeled red sandals.

Lively music floated up from a white gazebo close to the edge of the lake. Her steps, as she neared the gazebo, were captured by the rhythm and she walked in time to the music—right up to the knot of onlookers.

"Hi, Carole, I was hoping you'd be here today." He was very tall, very deeply tanned, and his blond hair was bleached almost colorless by the sun.

"Hi, Stephen," she greeted a fellow employee from the bank. "Did Ramona come with you?"

"Yes, my dear wife's talking with James right now." She spotted them sitting on an old-fashioned wooden bench at the rim of the floor. His grin was quite pleasant and friendly. "I enjoy coming to the Bensons' every year. I see people here that I see only once a year. Some of the guests come all the way from Dallas and Houston. See that couple over there? He's an oilman from Houston. They never miss this party. And there's one of the Dallas Cowboys and his wife." Almost as an afterthought, he added, "Did you come with Daniel?"

"There are no secrets in this family, are there?"

"After all, Carole, you can't go out to a public place with the bachelor pastor of a church and not expect someone to notice. Anything serious between you two?"

"Your mother wouldn't happen to be Teletype Tillie, would she?" Her irritation was apparent, but she answered his question. "No, we're just friends."

"I didn't mean to upset you. I was just curious, like most folks. He's really a fine man and you're a particularly nice woman. You'd make a super pair."

Raising her hand in silent protest, she said a little tartly, "Spare me the editorial comments."

He said no more on the subject, but Carole noticed a strange gleam in his eyes just as a familiar voice spoke behind her, "Hello, there." With a sinking feeling in her heart, she turned to see Daniel's shining brown eyes.

As he took her arm and led her to a more private place, Carole felt a moment of panic, but quickly recovered her composure as she remembered her bargain with herself.

"I wondered if I'd see you here today. Are you having a good time?" His smile was dazzling.

"Oh, yes, I always enjoy the Labor Day party. My biggest problem is deciding which activity I want to join in first," she said.

"Doesn't your date have any suggestions?"

"I don't need a date for this party," she mockingly told him. "That way I get to do all the things I really want to do."

"Independent little thing, aren't you? So you really just didn't want to come with *me*."

"Don't you think we've given people enough to talk about for a while? You might think about *me*. I don't want to be labeled as 'the pastor's date.' All you had to do was go out with me one time, and people had us tagged as a steady item." There was no way to argue with her statement. "You'll scare off all my other beaus." She smiled disarmingly.

The music ended and they moved over to the benches.

"Hi, Betty. Is James *still* talking with Ramona?"

Carole's teasing manner drew a pout and a frown from Betty. "I hope I haven't been jilted," she moaned playfully. "That would certainly end the party on a bad note." She scooted over to make room for Carole and Daniel.

Betty nudged Carole and asked in a low voice, "Out with Daniel again? Is there anything serious . . . ?"

"No, there isn't," she interrupted. Then hoping to distract her friend, she asked, "Did you see the Dallas Cowboy and his wife over there?"

"Oh." Betty's eyes searched the crowd for the object of the sudden new topic of conversation. "Oh, yeah, the guy that looks like a mountain wearing boots. Good-looking, too, isn't he? And there comes another good-looking fellow. I'm married to that one."

Daniel ended a conversation with Stephen and turned to Carole. "Hey, they're starting up the Cotton-eyed Joe."

"Daniel, look!" Her eyes twinkled, for the heavily-muscled football player had claimed a new partner.

Tillie was decked out in full Western gear. Her pipestem body was encased in brand-new jeans and a pearl-buttoned yellow cowboy shirt. Red ringlets dangled from beneath a brown Stetson hat, and in place of her orthopedic shoes, she wore yellow lizard-skin boots.

Tillie may have looked like a bad Western wear ad, but she was a skillful folk dancer. She led the long double line of couples around the floor as the band played. Though her mouth was closed tightly in a thin line, she kept up with the best of them.

Carole and Daniel shared a smile, and he asked, "Why don't we go for a swim in the pool?"

Measuring him with cautious eyes and deciding there were no hooks in his offer, she decided to take a chance. Besides, a cool dip would be refreshing in this late summer heat. "All right," she conceded.

They walked back up toward the rambling old house. It had a genteel look about it, but it was not overpowering like many of the large houses in the area. Rather, it looked well lived in and loved.

"I wonder what it would be like to live in a house like this," Carole speculated.

"Oh, I imagine it's pretty much like any other house. But I don't think too much about things like that, since I know that unless I strike oil in my backyard, I'll never have an opportunity to find out."

They walked up the steps of the house and entered the great hallway.

"Men's dressing room, this way; ladies', that way. See you in a few minutes." Daniel started down the long hall.

Daniel was executing a shallow dive when Carole reappeared. She was wearing a two-piece swimsuit in bright shades of blue. As Daniel surfaced, flinging the water from his face, he gave her an appraising look, but refrained from commenting on her appearance.

Her hair was pulled back into the ponytail she usually wore when swimming. She dived cleanly off the side of the pool and swam over to him. They paddled around companionably for a while before climbing up on the side of the pool to dry off and have something to drink. He handed her a tall, frosted glass of lemonade as she dried her face with a brightly colored towel.

"I do love water." Carole turned her face up to the sun and closed her eyes. "It reminds me of the beach."

"Do you like swimming in the Gulf?" He watched her closely over the rim of his glass.

"Mmm, my folks used to take us on vacation down there when we were children. But I loved looking for sharks' teeth almost better."

"Sharks' teeth! You're teasing me, of course."

"No, they wash in all the time. You look for a place where the white mussel shells have eddied in and just stand there and pick them up. Honest," she said earnestly at his look of disbelief. "I have jars of them at home. Remind me and I'll show them to you sometime."

"Now that would be a new line. 'Come on over and I'll show you my sharks' teeth.'"

She couldn't help laughing at the ridiculous suggestion.

"Well, you've got to admit it's more sophisticated than etchings." His grin was wicked as he attempted to keep the laughter alive between them.

Uneasiness slipped like a cloak over Carole with the turn of the conversation, and she tried to move back to safer, more impersonal grounds.

"Race you across!" she shouted.

Without waiting for Carole to line up beside him, Daniel made a clean dive into the pool and stroked cleanly for the other side.

"Now I've seen everything," she complained as he pulled led himself up on the side of the pool. "A cheating preacher! I can't wait to hear your sermon next Sunday. I hope it isn't on living honestly in a dishonest world."

"Come on across and I'll make it up to you."

"Again? I think maybe I'd better point out something to you that may have escaped your awareness." She looked at the very handsome man across the pool and saw him watching her intently. That familiar warmth started in the pit of her stomach and radiated outwardly. Helpless to stem the flood of feelings, she concentrated on her sermonette. "You have managed quite handily to do whatever you like, quickly following up with confessions of guilt and a fast atonement. I thought the object of repentance was a change in the person."

"Am I getting sunburned, or is this a manly blush spreading across my face?" He jumped into the water and paddled over to her and, with a strong push, pulled himself up beside her. "You're the most frustrating woman I've ever met, but there are times I know exactly how Adam felt before God gave him Eve." His eyes reached out and held hers in a close embrace.

For a suspended moment in time, she felt his searing loneliness, for it mirrored her own. Only one who has lost can know that ache to the fullest degree, and she longed to pull him against her and ease that hurt. She saw his face moving closer to hers, the mouth slightly open. She shifted her head to meet the angle of his lips. Somewhere a warning buzzer went off in the back of her head, but it was only an annoying sound, devoid of meaning. It grew louder as he

65

drew nearer, and she shook her head to push it away, causing his kiss to land on her cheek. His touch brought her back to reality. Confusion was her primary feeling now, and to cover it she said, "We aren't the only two people on earth, you know," and moved to put a safe distance between them.

"Of course," he said gruffly. "But if I ever saw a bright, shiny red apple, you're it." There was a long pause while they both sorted their thoughts, then Daniel said, "Are you hungry? It looks as though the big barbeque is about to begin. Why don't we get dressed and join the feast."

"That sounds like a fine idea."

As she tugged at her swimsuit in the dressing room, her thoughts seemed as hard to shed as the clingy, wet material. *Why did he try to kiss me? We both agreed—never again! I don't understand what's happening.* In the most secluded chamber of her heart, a tiny flame of hope sparked. *Maybe, just maybe I can handle this, after all.* And then fear slammed the door, snuffing out the fragile light.

## CHAPTER 5

DANIEL AND CAROLE found a small table for their supper at the edge of a grove of water oaks. A breeze played through the treetops and around their legs. People were seated at little tables, set up at random on the grounds, giving a sense of privacy to each group. Knowing the other people present gave them general topics of conversation, but the intimate setting encouraged more personal sharing.

"Are you having a good time?" Daniel asked.

"Yes, of course. Why do you ask?"

"I just wanted you to verify what I see. I told you I'm terrific at Labor Day parties."

"The thing I like most about you is your modesty," she said.

"And my humility," he added as he ducked his head in a parody of meekness. Then he straightened and looked deeply into her eyes. "I like being with you."

"I like being with you, too, Daniel."

"Will you let today count as my atonement for the mistake I made out at the lake?"

The intensity of his gaze made her look away. "Yes, I suppose so. But I have to know something, Daniel. How could you be so casual Sunday morning after—after what happened?"

"What did you expect me to do? I was assuming you didn't want the entire congregation to know. It was very difficult for me, but I have learned how to slip into the role of a pastor and put my personal feelings aside. That's the only way I can make it through the funeral of a dear friend . . . or treat a woman I have kissed so passionately as just another member of my congregation."

"I dreaded going to that service. I was sure everyone knew where we had been and what we had done. When Tillie cornered me outside, I nearly died. If Joyce hadn't spilled that water on her, I don't know what I would have said." She laughed at the memory of the scene.

"I missed that, but I heard about it. Joyce is a good friend to you." They slipped into a momentary silence. Then Daniel began haltingly. "Carole, I'm not sorry about what happened out there, or at the pool, either. I *am* sorry that I promised you it would never happen again. I want it to. I've been dreaming about it almost nightly."

"Don't, Daniel. I don't want to talk about it," she said in panic.

"Don't pretend you didn't feel something for me. I felt your fire and your need. Perhaps if I hadn't . . ." he began ruefully.

"Daniel, don't," she interrupted. "There's no point in going on about what can never be."

"You might as well try to hold back the dawn," he said confidently. "I have no intentions of just letting you slip through my fingers."

"The decision is not yours to make," she said firmly. "It is very arrogant of you to assume as much." Her eyes flashed dangerously. "And if you don't stop this nonsense, I'll leave."

"Run, rabbit, run," he said tauntingly. "You can run now, but I'll just pursue you. I'm sure everyone would enjoy that spectacle."

"You wouldn't dare." But seeing the determination in his face, she knew he would. "Why are you doing this?"

"I want you to give me a chance. You're trying to throw away what could be a beautiful relationship. I told you the other night, things don't have to be the way they were with you and Samuel. We're not children. This is another congregation. You'd be safe with me. Just give us a chance."

His earnestness pulled mightily at the chamber door of her heart—and it yielded.

"All right, Daniel, we'll give it a try." The words came out almost in a whisper. Her eyes pleaded with him. "But please go slowly with me. Let me get used to the idea of loving again. If only you were a carpenter . . ."

"But I'm not." He took her hand and lifted it to his lips. The kiss was warm, but when he turned her hand over and kissed the inside of her palm, she felt as if lightning had struck her.

"It's time, Carole, to live and love again."

She pulled her hand back. "It's also time to stop what you're doing. Someone might see us."

"Is that the real reason?" His smile was warm and intimate, but he leaned back in his chair.

"Daniel, you're downright dangerous," she declared.

"Only where you're concerned. Let me ask you one more question." She steeled herself for anything.

"Are you going to eat that piece of apple pie?"

Chuckling, she pushed the pie toward him. "How could I refuse such a sincere request? But it will cost you one more question."

"Hmm. Esau sold his birthright for only a bowl of pottage. I think I got a better deal."

"Is there anything between you and Mrs. Willingham?"

"Only the symphony, my dear. And she definitely plays a poor second fiddle to you."

She was to savor that evening for the rest of her life.

The music drifting in from the gazebo to their private place was dreamy and romantic. As Daniel beckoned, she moved into his arms with a new awareness. His body, so close to hers, still made her feel as though an electric current was charging her senses, but she wasn't afraid now. She didn't fight her response. As they sat on a grassy spot far from the crowd, the trees swayed, echoing their serenity.

He leaned down to put his lips on her forehead, moving them back and forth in a gentle caress. She lifted her face up to his and offered her mouth willingly. He kissed her carefully, tasting the sweetness of her. She gave, not in wild passion, but in a soft surrender—a gentle giving of her whole self. For Carole it was the ultimate trust. She had opened the door to her life and let Daniel in.

The sun slipped through her bedroom window and smiled at her. Without opening her eyes, she stretched her arms high over her head and twisted in a waking movement. Rolling over and lifting herself out of bed, she put on a brightly colored caftan to match her mood and headed for the kitchen.

She was just pouring steamy coffee into her yellow cup when the phone rang.

"Good morning!" said Daniel cheerfully.

"Good morning, yourself! Yours is the first voice I've heard. What a nice way to start the day."

"For me, too. I thought you'd be an early riser."

"Why?"

70

"Because of your name. A *carol* is a song, and *morgen* is German for morning. Carole Morgan—song of the morning."

Her delighted laugh spilled over into her words. "No one has ever told me that before. I'm touched."

"I thoroughly research a woman's name before I fall in love with her. Names are most important, you know," he said teasingly.

"Well, Daniel, you certainly were brave to enter the lion's den of my life."

His laugh was rich and deep. "The reason I called was to get a corner on the market of your evening."

"What did you have in mind?"

"How about supper at my house tonight?"

"You want to check out my culinary skills?"

"Nope, I'm going to treat *you.*"

"Scrambled eggs and bacon, huh?"

"Hey, I'm a good cook. I'll come get you about seven. Okay?" His eagerness was disarming.

"Wouldn't it be more practical for me to just drive over there myself?"

"That's not the way a proper courtship should be run."

"In the interest of economy of time and gas, we can allow this one breach of etiquette."

"You'll recognize me. I'll be the one in the frilly apron."

"Then I'll bring the after-dinner chocolates," she laughed.

"Make them cream-filled. Say, this courtship is off to a good start."

"See you at seven."

"Don't be late."

"That's just like a man—bossy—even in a frilly apron. I have to go to the office now. Some people have to work two jobs, you know. Bye."

As she refilled her cup, she tried to imagine Daniel in an apron. The idea kept her laughing all the way to her office.

Carole was normally cheerful at the bank, but even her secretary noticed the special spring in her step as she entered her office.

"Morning, Boss."

"*Guten morgen,*" said Carole, smiling.

"Meaning?" asked the puzzled young woman.

"Oh, it's just German for 'good morning'," she said off-handedly. "Is my agenda for the day ready?"

"Yes, here it is."

"Ah, Sandy, would you call the Candy Box and order a box of their fanciest cream-filled chocolates for me? I'll pick them up on my way home."

"Do you want them gift-wrapped?"

Carole's smile was positively dazzling. "What a fine idea. Better make that two boxes of their best chocolates. I had a wonderful time at the Bensons' party."

Sandy walked out of the office, raising a curious eyebrow, but without questioning her further.

The busy day went quickly and Carole was soon headed home for a quick bath and a change of clothes. She considered taking flowers, too, but decided that would be carrying their joke a little too far.

When Daniel opened the door, she was almost disappointed that the promised apron was missing.

"Come on in," he invited. "You're right on time."

"I couldn't wait to see your apron."

"Ah, I've already finished my cooking. You just missed it."

She followed him through the entrance hall and walked into the den. The house was large and fairly old, reflecting a bachelor's lifestyle. Everything was extremely practical, and she noticed that he had a good eye for art. An oversized seascape hung over the leather couch. It reminded her of the Texas Gulf Coast with its large sand dunes, laced with tall strands of grass and grayish-colored sand.

"This looks like a Galveston Island scene from my childhood," she remarked.

"Oh, I've never been to the coast. I just saw that in a gallery in Austin and it appealed to me. I've had it for several years."

She turned from the picture and handed him the gift-wrapped candy.

"For me? Oh, you shouldn't have, unless they're cream-filled, of course." Grinning, he unwrapped the package and nodded his approval of her choice. "We can have these with coffee later. Sit down and make yourself comfortable."

She settled down into a deep easy chair and looked around. There was much in the room that revealed Daniel's interests. She saw floor-to-ceiling bookcases filled with books on a wide variety of subjects. Tucked rather obscurely in one part of the shelf were several sports trophies.

"What are the trophies for?" she called to the kitchen.

"Oh, baseball, mostly. Remnants of my sem days," Daniel replied as he came around the corner, carrying a tray of colorful raw vegetables and a bowl of creamy dip. Placing the tray on a low table in front of her, he plopped down on the floor, very much at ease. "I still play on the church league softball team. We're third in the league right now. Do you like baseball?" He looked up at her and she was again struck by his rugged good looks.

"Of course. I grew up playing sandlot ball myself. In college I got interested in tennis, and I still play regularly."

"I'll have to check out your backhand one of these days," he teased. "I enjoy tennis, too. The coffee should be about ready—are you?'' He rose as he asked the question, and she put down the raw cauliflower she had just chosen.

"Let's take these vegetables with us."

The table was set attractively and he helped her with her chair.

"I hope you like poached liver," he said as he carried in a hot dish to the table. He saw the unguarded dismay on her face and burst into laughter.

"Lucky for you I fixed an old-fashioned southern meal, then. I can see you definitely don't like liver."

"Ah—not poached," she stammered.

"Here we are. Fried pork chops, baked potatoes, black-eyed peas, and, of course, the raw vegetables. I was going to bake a southern tea cake, too, but I was short of time. Hope you like lime sherbet." He proudly sat down at the table and beamed as she enjoyed, and complimented, each dish.

"I hate to sound like a female chauvinist, but you really are an excellent cook."

"And I'm glad you aren't one of those women who pick at their food. I hate it when people are constantly dieting."

"I'll just play an extra set of tennis tomorrow. Would you care to take me on? I play to win." The challenge was irresistible.

"You're on. Loser buys dinner. I play to win, too." He smiled, but she caught the undercurrent of his next words. "We'll make a good match. Just wait and see."

The kitchen was soon neat and clean. She felt an awkward moment when they had finished that activity, but Daniel smoothly moved them into the den for coffee and more conversation. They talked for hours, finding they had much more in common than Carole had suspected.

"Daniel, I really should be going. I have an important tennis match tomorrow, and I'll need my sleep. I've got a tough opponent."

"I'd rather you viewed him as a persistent one. I do intend to be persistent, you know."

She stood up to leave and he walked her to the door. They were standing very close, saying their good-nights. It felt very natural moving into the circle of his arms, leaning against him. His mouth on hers was already familiar, and so was the restrained passion she felt flowing from him.

"You are already so dear to me," he murmured against her mouth. "I won't rush you, or push you. I want you to come to me of your own free will." She started to speak, but his mouth once again gently took the breath from her body. They parted and he walked her out into the cool evening, tucking her into the car.

"Take it easy going home." His boyish grin broke out, "I don't want any excuses when we play tennis tomorrow . . . love!"

"Ugh!" was her comment as she backed into the street.


They split the sets in tennis.

"I told you we were well-matched," declared Daniel.

"So, who buys the dinner?"

"We could go Dutch," offered Daniel teasingly.

"Some gentleman you are."

They headed for the terrace of the club to cool off with frosty glasses of tea.

"Yoo-hoo, Pastor. Yoo-hoo," Tillie, clad in tennis togs, yelled from across the courts.

"Hello, Tillie," called Daniel, and in a lower voice he urged Carole, "Head straight for the car." He propelled her at a normal pace to the parking lot.

"Are we going to spend most of our time dodging her?" Carole asked.

"No, I just wasn't ready to face a barrage of questions about us yet," he replied.

"Whether *we* talk to her or not, she has something to talk about."

"I know that, but I'm not giving her any more ammunition than I have to."

"Daniel, I am not going to live like this," she stated flatly.

"Don't be silly, Carole. She's only one person. The whole congregation isn't like that. You just work around the few who are. You don't have to like her, just love her." His last statement struck Carole as totally illogical.

"What?"

"Love her. Just care about what happens to her."

"I understand what you're saying. But, you see, I have a choice: I don't *have* to deal with her. And you're conveniently forgetting about the Millers. Now *there's* a wonderful couple," she threw in sarcastically.

"You're letting this get all out of proportion." He was trying to be patient.

"No, Daniel. I'm recalling with alarming clarity what it was like. As part of the congregation, I could just turn them off. As your wife, I would be a focal point for them."

"I haven't asked you yet," he replied evenly.

"Well, don't." Carole's Irish ancestry raised its angry head, but she stifled it. They drove on in silence, neither looking at the other. As he stopped the car, she quickly jumped out.

"Good-by, Daniel." The slam of the car door emphasized the finality of her words. She walked quickly up the sidewalk and gave the front door a satisfying slam. Two doors in a row left her feeling a little better. She heard the roar of the car as Daniel drove away. *Well, that's that,* she realized, and was surprised when she felt only relief.

That evening she cleaned out closets, discarding useless items. She was ruthless in her choices, tossing them out with the same authority she had used in tossing away her life with Daniel.

She woke up tired the next morning—tired but confident she had done the right thing.

Carole made a valiant effort to act completely normal at the office, but she didn't get very far.

"Morning, Boss." It was Sandy's usual greeting.

"I wish you'd quit calling me 'Boss'," she snapped.

"Sorry, Mrs. Morgan." Sandy looked closely at her face. "Anything wrong?"

"No, Sandy." The short answer was definitely a storm warning.

"Here's your daily agenda." Sandy beat a fast retreat to a safer area.

Carole was aware that Sandy was walking a wide circle around her that day, doing nothing to irritate her. *Everyone has a bad day once in a while,* she rationalized. Her gloomy mood made for a long eight hours. Fortunately for the bank and its customers, Carole kept busy with paperwork. Finally, the clock moved its dragging hands to five.

"That's all for today, Sandy. I'm on my way home."

"Yes, ma'am." Sandy sighed with relief. Carole heard the sigh, but pointedly ignored it and left abruptly.

Once home, she felt some of her tension ease, grateful that she didn't have to interact with anyone for the rest of the evening.

After changing into blue shorts and a soft shirt, she padded into the kitchen. She had a hard time finding something to eat, but finally settled for a chef's salad. Chopping up the vegetables was tedious, but forced her attention from the thoughts in her mind.

Carole carried the salad to the solace of the cool patio. The quiet irritated her, so she brought out a radio and listened to a local station. "Don't they play decent music on any of these stations anymore?" she complained, flipping the dial up and down the channels.

"What's the matter with me?" she questioned herself aloud. "I know I did the right thing." Her voice was firm. "I've been out so much lately that I've simply gotten used to being with people all the time. Well, dear," she chided, "you'd better get accustomed to the way it used to be." Nevertheless, she kept waiting for the phone to ring; dreading it, yet wanting it.

She went to bed early to end the awful day. Carole tossed and turned, but as she finally began nodding off to sleep, she whispered, "Dear God, grant me peace again."

## CHAPTER 6

CAROLE GRADUALLY BEGAN to settle into her former life. The days were livable because she was busy at work, but the evenings were long and difficult. She filled them as best she could.

Tonight would be easier, for she was going to spend it with Joyce. It was a little after seven-thirty when she heard the doorbell ring, and went to answer it with a light heart.

"Hi! Come on in," she invited.

"Sorry I'm late. The traffic threw me off schedule. You're looking chipper."

"Thank you. So are you." She led Joyce to the den where she had laid out some snacks.

"I see you've been doing some cooking," said Joyce as she sat down beside the low table, and sampled a chocolate éclair.

"I've had a little more time for that sort of thing these days."

"You mean, now that you've broken off with Daniel?"

"So you're up-to-date on all the latest news."

79

"I would rather have heard it from you first," said Joyce a little testily.

"I'm sorry, Joyce, I guess I wasn't ready to talk about it yet."

"Do you still love him?"

"No, yes . . . I mean I still care about him as a friend." Carole flicked an imaginary crumb from her camel slacks.

"I can tell by your definite answer that you've thought this all out very carefully, and you still don't know what you're doing."

"Oh, Joyce, I'm so miserable. How did I get myself into this mess? One minute I'm mad at him, the next minute I'm so lonely for him I could die, and the very next, I know that it would never work for us. It doesn't matter. He hasn't even called."

"Have you thought about calling him and apologizing?"

"Yes, but then I decided it would only prolong everything."

"Prolong what?"

"It's never going to work. I don't want to be a pastor's wife. When I'm with him, I forget all the things I've learned. I guess I should thank Tillie for bringing it all to my attention again—the old witch."

"Who are you mad at?"

"Everyone but you, I guess."

"Carole, do you love him?" Joyce persisted.

"Yes, but I'm even more afraid of what he is. As long as I stay away from him, I can keep a perspective on things. Then I see him and I become a dopy schoolgirl. Maybe the best thing to do would be to change churches. I can't bear the thought of seeing him every Sunday."

"That sounds like a good idea."

"But all my friends are there," protested Carole. "Why should I have to give them up because of him?"

"That's true. It wouldn't be fair. Maybe *he'll* move."

"Now that's a possibility I hadn't considered."

"Of course, he's only been here a short time, and pastors don't usually move that quickly. If he's as miserable as you are, though, he might consider it."

"Is he miserable, too?"

Joyce dropped her eyes. "He didn't look miserable when I saw him with Mrs. Willingham at the restaurant the other night."

"Mrs. Willingham? He took her out? That rat, that, that . . ."

"Son of a Siberian sea cook?" Joyce added helpfully.

"How dare he! Why we haven't even been apart a week, and he's already dating someone else!"

"Well, I'm certainly glad we've proved that you don't care for him any more." Suddenly Carole saw the grin on Joyce's face.

"You tricked me! He didn't take her out. You just told me that to see what I would say."

"It worked, didn't it? Green is a becoming shade for you, Carole. Suits you better than blue. Well, kid, what are you going to do now?"

"Become a nun."

"Still running," Joyce sighed.

"But Daniel isn't running after *me*. It's just as well. He's obviously made the choice for both of us, and I know it's the right one. I'm going to change churches and stay away from men. And I'm not going to that dumb convention, either!"

"Even though you still care for him?"

"Even though I still care for him—a little. It really is for the best. My head told me that from the beginning."

"But not your heart?"

"Those two will just have to learn to live together. I've

made my choice. Thanks, Joyce, for helping.'' Relief erased the crinkled brow.

"Don't thank me. *I* think you're making a royal mistake. But it's your life, not mine. I'll love you no matter what you decide. Want me to introduce you to my cousin?'' she asked as she rose to leave.

"Joyce, you're a nut.''

"Yeah, but I am serious about my cousin. I'll call you later in the week and see how you feel about it. It would do you good to get out again.''

"All right. Call me later. Maybe I do need a night out.'' She walked Joyce to the door and they exchanged farewells.

Several days later when the phone rang she answered it, expecting to hear the latest lecture from Joyce.

"Carole.'' Her heart literally skipped a beat as she recognized Daniel's voice.

"Yes.'' It came out a little breathlessly.

"I need to see you. How about dinner?'' The question sounded a little husky.

"No, I don't think that's a good idea.'' There was a moment of silence.

"I need to talk with you. Would you come to my office for a while then?'' His request held a promise that was undeniably enticing.

She felt herself weakening. "There's really no point, Daniel,'' she began.

"Just for a little while. Of course, if you're afraid . . .''

"I'm not afraid.'' The gauntlet had been thrown. "What time?'' She accepted the challenge.

"About seven-thirty.''

"I'll be there.''

She changed into a pair of dusky rose slacks with a matching sweater and drove to the church at the appointed time, feeling both anxious and vaguely excited.

She knocked on the door and entered at his invitation. Carole's head was high and she met his gaze steadily as Daniel rose from his chair to greet her. For one split second she realized she was on his turf, though she did have the advantage of leaving at any given moment.

Daniel's study was a comfortable room, carpeted in deep red, with several chairs facing his oversized desk. Dark brown cabinets matched the bookshelves, which were filled with books on theology and related subjects.

"I'm glad you came." He indicated a chair for her and she sat down, slightly tensed.

"Well, what did you want to talk about?" Her question was crisp and businesslike.

"Right to the heart of the matter," he quipped in an effort to lighten the atmosphere. She smiled faintly in spite of herself. He stood up and spanned the distance between them in two long strides before dropping into a chair beside her.

"I think we're back to square one. I don't think you're being honest with yourself, Carole. I want you to give us a chance." She started to speak, but he held up his hand in a gesture of silence. Then he used that hand to take hers. "Come with me." He led her, unprotesting, into the church. The sun had almost set, bathing the sanctuary in a soft golden glow. They stood to one side looking toward the stained-glass windows over the altar.

"When I get discouraged I come in here to pray." He smiled a rueful smile. "I've been here often lately." His eyes scrutinized the blazing window carefully. "I told the Lord how lonely I am. Reminded Him, even, how He had felt sorry for Adam in his solitude." Daniel's gaze shifted from the window to Carole's eyes. "When my wife died I thought no one could ever possibly understand my grief. Only someone who has experienced the death of someone dear has any concept of the complexities of that sadness."

Carole nodded her head in agreement. "I know."

He took her hand and pulled her with him into a pew. They sat side by side, looking straight ahead at the brass cross hanging over the altar, gleaming in the honeyed light, and shared the serenity of the sanctuary.

"Carole, I was very pleased to see you that Sunday. You were so beautiful, so alive." He looked at his hands clasped loosely on his knees. "You made me realize that there was a cold stone where my heart once had been. I didn't *want* to feel anything for so long. And then, there you were." He turned his head slightly to look at her in profile. "That afternoon in the cabin was the first time I'd kissed a woman since Ellen died. You started the thaw in my heart. But I knew you didn't want to get mixed up with another minister, so I tried to forget about it." A deep chuckle accompanied his next confession. "Obviously, that wasn't too bright an idea!" She smiled with him. "I did all the things I knew to do to forget you, but you were imprinted on my heart . . . Carole, look at me." She turned to look into his deep brown eyes, eyes that touched her very soul with the love shining out of them.

"I believe that God has given us to each other, he said. "We've both suffered the sorrow of losing someone we loved. Knowing how precious it really is can make our love stronger. I can't go on another day without knowing that you will marry me."

Without a word Carole moved into his arms and kissed him tenderly. "Oh, Daniel," she whispered.

He kissed her sweet mouth again, languorously taking and giving joy. His arms wrapped around her as if to shield her from any possible unhappiness.

She pulled away and lay her head on his broad chest, hearing the steady beating of his heart. His face nuzzling her hair brought a soft smile to her freshly kissed lips. Raising those lips to him, she said, "Daniel I love you with all my heart. I believe, too, that God has given us to each other. I'm not afraid anymore, not with both of you on my side."

Huskily he told her, "I've stormed heaven for your love, Carole."

Her eyes crinkled with happiness. "I hope you won't regret having those prayers answered."

"Never! I love you too much." The words, interspersed with gentle kisses, were whispered against her mouth, her hair.

She tried to move out of the circle of his arms, but he tightened them around her. "I was just going back into your office," she chided gently.

"Promise you won't disappear."

"Not a chance." Her face radiated the happiness she felt.

"You look lovely in the moonlight," he said softly.

"But, we're not . . . Oh, you! Life with you certainly won't be dull."

"Not a chance," he echoed. "Now, let's get down to some important business." He rubbed his hands together in anticipation and led her into the study.

"Please be seated, Mrs. Morgan. Now when did you say you wanted this wedding performed? My calendar is free tomorrow." She laughed. "Too soon? Don't let me rush you, but how about the day after?"

"Will it always be this wonderful?" she asked, still laughing.

"Always." His eyes were opened wide in excitement, accentuating his handsome face, and her heart reached out to store away every loving and beloved feature of it.

"I think I could get everything done in three weeks. Would that be all right with you?"

"No, but my practical side tells me that would be best.

I'll need time to get someone to fill my pulpit while we're on our honeymoon, and I need to do quite a bit of rescheduling of my meetings. What a happy problem!" He grinned at her. "The convention should be a lot more interesting since I can introduce you as my soon-to-be wife!"

There was a tiny worry line over her brows as she said, "This is all so sudden. Do you think the people will approve?"

He turned his head slightly and looked at her earnestly. "They'll be delighted. Even if they aren't, this is my life. Remember, you promised to stop looking over your shoulder," he warned gently. "Now about the ceremony: I'd like my best friend to do the honors. You remember my classmate, Pete Bastien?"

"I know him, though I didn't know he was your classmate. That was a little before my time," she said. "But it's fine with me. I like him. Of course, I want Joyce to be my matron of honor."

"I couldn't tell you how many weddings I've performed over the years, but it certainly seems strange, making the arrangements for my own," he said sheepishly. "I had forgotten just how much planning was involved." He grinned "I was beginning to think I'd never get the chance—again." Love warmed his eyes as he gazed at his bride-to-be. "Will you go with me to choose your ring, or shall I surprise you?"

Her eyes crinkled in a merry laugh. "I don't think an engagement ring is necessary. I'd barely have time to wear it! But if you insist on giving me one, I'd like to go with you," she said shyly. The buying of rings suddenly struck her as a very intimate time, for it was the epitome of the symbol of their new love and the life they would soon be sharing.

"Since we are legally engaged to be wed, do you think

we could continue this meeting in the surroundings of our home-to-be?"

"All right." She began searching her purse for her car key.

"Ah, I meant at *my* home." He paused, noticing her perplexity. "Hey, maybe we have a little more talking to do," he said with an embarrassed chuckle.

"Yes, I guess we do." She closed her purse and waited in the heavy moment of silence that followed for a way to tell him that she wanted to stay in her own home.

"I think we have a real problem here, unless you can answer one question in the affirmative," he said flatly. She took a deep breath. "Do you have enough room for all the books I have at my house?" The twinkle in his eyes told her that the brief moment of tension was over.

"I think I can accommodate you," she said with relief.

"I saw you automatically reaching for your keys, Carole, and realized that home means only one place for you. For me, home is where *you* are, trite as that might sound."

She walked into the warm circle of his arms and laid her head on his well-muscled chest, wrapping her arms around him. "You are not only astute, you are the kindest man I've ever known."

"Let's go home, my love."

In the intimacy of the home they would share, they made the rest of their wedding plans.

By the end of the next day, Carole had accomplished a great deal. She had finally found time to sit down on her patio for a breather when the phone rang at her elbow. "I was hoping it would be you," she said warmly as she heard Daniel's voice on the other end of the line.

"I just called to say good night. Happy?" His voice was surfeited with joy.

She held up her hand. The large cluster of diamonds gleamed in the twilight. "I'm feeling a little guilty for letting you talk me into such an expensive ring. But I do love it."

"I wanted you to have the best, my love. I don't ever plan to buy another wedding set, and I wanted to go out in a blaze of glory," he said firmly. "I figured that if I had enough invested in you, you wouldn't back out on me," he countered.

"It does look a little ostentatious," she started, only to be interrupted by a warning voice.

"Carole."

"Yes, dear, I hear you. I shall wallow in my luxury. But it has given me big ideas about what I can expect from my rich husband."

"Only the best, my dear, only the best. Good night, my love."

"Good night," she echoed softly, and replaced the phone reluctantly in its cradle.

The days spent themselves in a maze of activity. But Carole made sure she took time to do one important thing. She told Daniel about it rather factually one evening as they sat together comparing tasks accomplished.

"You did what?" Dismay clouded his rugged features.

"I resigned my job," she repeated a little more firmly.

"Would you tell me why?" He was clearly at a loss to explain this action.

"Because I want to spend all my energies being your wife. You know how hard it is to be a working wife, or you should," she said defensively.

He leaned back in his deep-cushioned chair and sighed deeply. "Do you think that will be enough for you?" His concern was genuine.

"Of course, it will be. I don't need anything but you, Daniel. My job was a means of support. I don't need or want anything that can take away from our life together." Her face pleaded for acceptance.

"I know, Carole. It's Okay. It just caught me by surprise. I guess I think this is something we should have decided together. We've been discussing everything all the way down the line. It's all right," he repeated.

Her manner was subdued. "I meant this for a happy surprise. I never thought that you'd be anything but pleased. Most men would have been. I'm sorry." She curled up against him on the arm of the chair. "I didn't mean to spoil things."

"You didn't spoil anything. Why, now I'll have my own one-woman harem, waiting on me hand and foot." He kissed her lightly. "Let's get on with the rest of the plans—and there is the convention to think about." His tone indicated that he had already dismissed the unfortunate incident from his mind.

But Carole made a silent vow never to make that mistake again.

## CHAPTER 7

CAROLE TRIED TO REMEMBER her reflection in the mirror just before she had left the house. Was this dress her most becoming one, or just passable? Maybe she should have gotten a haircut, maybe even changed the style. *I want to look my best for Daniel,* she rationalized her new vanity. And that was true. But it was vastly more complicated than she cared to admit. Now that she had nothing but time on her hands as the car sped to Dallas, the whole thing came sweeping back into her mind.

The initial excitement of the beginning of the trip had waned, and the small talk had run out. She looked at Daniel, but he seemed totally absorbed in maneuvering the car around two big trucks. Joyce was in the back seat trying her best to be nice to Mr. Miller. What a terrible shock that had been. Mr. Miller filling in at the last minute for Mel Johnson. Carole had almost refused to go when she found out he would be the fourth person.

"How in the world am I supposed to enjoy myself with that walking negative attitude close behind?" she had fumed at Daniel when he told her the news. "He's not a thorn in my side. He's not even a millstone around my neck. He's a, he's a—"

"Never mind, I get the picture. Now, Carole," explained Daniel patiently, "we can let him ruin this trip for us, or we can fool him and have a good time in spite of him." He looked hopefully at the enraged woman pacing back and forth.

"I'm as mad at you as I am at that—that man!"

"Me! What did I do?"

"Well, I know you couldn't prevent his going, but you could at least be mad that he is. I am so tired of your patient acceptance of everything!"

"Will you stop speaking in exclamation points and listen. It doesn't do any good to get mad every time things don't go your way. I just save my anger for the important things." He gave her a saintly smile.

"And you, my dear, are full of baloney." She crossed her arms and glared at him.

Silently he rose and stalked toward the door. He opened it a crack, then turned to speak to her. "You went too far this time, Carole. That was uncalled for, unnecessary, and unkind." He walked through the door and closed it with a great wham.

Carole grinned broadly and rushed for the door. Reaching for it, it swung toward her with Daniel's hand on the other door knob. "You did it! You got mad! Yea!" she cried.

He wore his chagrin with great dignity. "Yes, I did."

"How do you feel?"

"Foolish. Not for getting mad," he amended, "but for getting sucked into your web. You know," he said with admiration in his voice, "I've sidestepped some of the best goat-getters in the world, but you seem to be able to get to me at will. Somewhere there's a huge hole in my armor where you're concerned." He walked to her and took her in his arms, kissing the tip of her nose.

"Perhaps it's the price of love." She grinned up at him. "Tell me the truth, aren't you really angry that old Miller is going to be there to see all and tell what he likes?"

"I'll admit I was disappointed at first. But then I sat down and figured it all out. He'll be in the car with us for roughly two-and-a-half to three hours en route to Dallas, and the same amount coming home. Six hours tops. The rest of the time we dodge him." Mischief gleamed from his dark eyes.

"Aren't you going to room with him, too?"

"Sure, but I get up very early, and I rarely go to bed before midnight. At least that will be my schedule during the convention. I figure I can stand anything as long as I know there will be an end to it. This endurance test will last only three days. And look at the opportunities! I can be with you alone for three whole days and nights." Seeing her lifted eyebrows, he added, "Well, at least part of the nights. I'll get a chance to introduce you as my future wife to all my old friends. Won't they be surprised!" His face was alight with the joy only anticipation can bring. "Are you excited about seeing your friends again?" He studied her face expectantly.

"Yes, of course I'll be glad to see them. I do feel a little nervous. After all it's been almost six years since I've been to a convention. Frankly I've avoided them like the plague," she said ruefully. Softly she added, "Now, I'll be going back as a minister's fiancée. I think maybe the world is round. Here I am again."

"Regrets?" He pulled her a little closer.

The question echoed in her mind, but she didn't want to deal with the answer yet. Did she regret that she had agreed to marry Daniel? No. She truly loved him. The fact that he was a minister was the crux of the matter, and no matter how she grappled with the problem, it remained shrouded in a cloud of apprehension.

Carole watched the pine-treed scenery subtly change to one dominated by oaks and scrub cedar. Dogwood dotted the timbered areas, until they moved into open pasture land. The closer they got to the metropolitan area of Dallas, the more open ranges she saw. It was a lovely drive any time of year and she felt her pulse quicken as the skyline of Dallas came into view. The traffic thickened as they turned onto the downtown exit that would take them to the hotel.

"I've never stayed at 'The Fairmont.' Have you?"

"Surely you jest. I'm just a pastor. This should be the best-attended convention in years. No one could resist saying they stayed at 'The Fairmont.' First-class all the way."

Carole heard Mr. Miller take up the conversation, commenting on the outlandishness of the church's picking up such an expensive tab, and she blocked out the rest of his complaint and concentrated on her own thoughts.

"You look absolutely gorgeous," Daniel said softly.

Gratitude shone in the look she turned to him. "Thanks, I needed that."

The huge hotel didn't seem special on the outside, but as they entered the lobby, Carole had to stifle a gasp. It was quietly elegant, done in red velvet. But it was the three-story chandelier suspended gracefully above the lobby and ablaze with lights that took her breath away.

The party went to the front desk to receive their room keys. The reservationist was harried, but seemed to be handling the crush of people well. Carole deliberately looked neither right nor left in an effort not to recognize anyone just yet.

"Thornton," said the man behind the desk. "Ah, here it is. Suite 1527."

"Uh, I don't need a suite. There are just two of us," corrected Daniel. "And then we need a double room for these two ladies."

"I'm sorry, sir. I have you booked for a suite for four. I think you will find that satisfactory. There are two bedrooms with a connecting sitting room. Both bedrooms have private baths, of course." Seeing Daniel's dismay, he added, "That's the only thing I can do for you, sir. We're booked solid." He handed the key to the bellhop in a gesture of dismissal.

Daniel grinned at the waiting trio and shrugged. "It seems we will be living in real luxury for the next three days and nights. Don't worry, it will all work out." Neither he nor Carole dared to look at Mr. Miller. But Joyce had an enormous grin on her face when they glanced her way.

"Conventions always start with a problem," Daniel cheerfully asssured them as they rode the swift elevator up into the tower. "Let's just consider it a challenge."

When Carole dared to steal a look at Mr. Miller's grim face, her heart sank into her new leather sling pumps. But the thought of staying so close to Daniel for the next few days stirred a warm response. She poked Joyce in the ribs in an effort to wipe the silly grin off her face.

*I'm sorry,* Joyce pantomimed. But the grin just wouldn't go away.

The bellhop unlocked the huge door and carried the luggage inside the room on the rolling rack. "These two doors lead to the bedrooms," he said, motioning to opposite ends of the sitting room.

"We'll take this one," Joyce said quickly and headed for the room on the left. Carole followed slowly, drinking in the lovely decor of the sitting room—done in rich gray and maroon. There was a large couch and several chrome directors' chairs, glass-topped coffee and side tables, and a

94

large table that could be used for dining. A graceful desk was positioned against one wall, and on the opposite wall was a floor-to-ceiling window with a spectacular view of Dallas. Mr. Miller walked over to the television console and flipped the switch. "Well, at least the TV works." It was all he said before walking into the bedroom he would share with Daniel.

Daniel tipped the bellhop and waved a cheerful good-by to Carole as they parted for their rooms. Carole heard the other bedroom door close with finality.

Joyce was stretched out full length on the queen-sized bed. "I think I could force myself to get used to living like this," she sighed. "Check out the bathroom," she ordered.

Obediently Carole entered the gleaming white room. Two plush velvet robes lay carefully folded and waiting. There was a white telephone, a bath scale, and a wicker clothes hamper. The inside of the cabinet held everything one would need for an extended stay. "Wow!"

"That's just what I said. Now look inside the armoire."

Inside was another television set and lots of room for any item one cared to store there. Carole plopped down in the deep cushioned chair by the floor-to-ceiling windows. "I'd hate to see the bill for these draperies."

"I'm thinking of just staying right here for the next three days and nights," purred Joyce. "Room service is just a touch away," she said and pointed to the bedside phone. Both of them jumped as the phones rang simultaneously in the bath and beside the bed. Joyce picked up the receiver. "Yes? For you, Carole. I think he's a tall, dark and handsome."

"Hello," she said.

"I feel silly calling you like this."

"Well, hello," she answered in a huskier voice. "I assume Mr. M. is standing right there."

"Yes, that's true," he answered perfunctorily.

"Rather cramps one's style, eh, Romeo."

"Yes," he answered, laughing. "How's your room?"

"Oh, it's all right if you like understated elegance and affluence."

"We need to get downstairs and register. Can you be ready in about five minutes?"

"Five minutes will be fine. I'll check to see if I can get my live-in maid to get off her, er, bed long enough to make it to the door." She made a face at Joyce.

"I'm eager to show you off." His excitement was contagious.

Her stomach did a remarkably large flip-flop, considering the confined area in which it had to work. "I'll be ready," she sighed, "Bye."

"But I've grown accustomed to this place already," groaned Joyce. "Okay, Okay, I'm moving. Slave-driver." But her eyes contradicted her words. She, too, was eager to begin the adventure.

Both women quickly smoothed their hair and checked their makeup. "Ready?" asked Carole before she nervously opened the door to the sitting room.

"Wait, Carole. I want you to know that just as soon us I can, I'll leave you and Daniel alone, but," she warned, "it's up to you to get rid of Miller. All I can do is run a little interference for you."

"Don't be silly. We both enjoy your company. Don't you dare just run off and leave us. There's nothing so lonely as attending a convention by oneself. Besides, someone has to look after *me,*" and she opened the door before Joyce could protest.

"Why don't we go get our badges and convention packets," Daniel suggested, rising from the couch.

"Good idea," said Mr. Miller. "Maybe they can

straighten out the problem with our room."

No one replied to that comment.

Carole felt the customary butterflies escape in her stomach as they rode the elevator down to the ballroom where the meetings were to be held. She felt Daniel's hand in hers and gave it a quick squeeze.

They almost made it to the registration desk before they saw anyone they knew.

"Daniel!" cried a deep voice.

"Harold! It's good to see you here. Let me introduce my lay delegates. Joyce Stohlman and Herbert Miller, one of my old classmates, Harold Wageman. And I imagine you remember Carole Morgan. I'm happy to say that Carole and I will be married very shortly." Daniel was positively beaming at Carole.

"How do you do," he said to Joyce and Mr. Miller. "Hello, Carole. It's been a long time since I last saw you. You're looking terrific. Married, huh? Well, congratulations! I'm really pleased for you both." There was no mistaking the genuine joy he expressed at their forthcoming marriage.

"Jo is around here some place. Just wait until I tell her your news. She'll be so happy for both of you!"

"Thanks, Harold. I'll watch for her." Carole was glad that she'd be seeing Jo—one of the "real" people she had known in the sisterhood of ministers' wives.

One fine spring day she and Jo had attended a large gathering of pastors' wives. As the ladies sat around in the parsonage living room talking babies and laundry problems, one of the women began telling a story about her husband. She began, "Pastor told me . . ." Immediately Jo had leaned over to Carole and whispered, "I wonder what she calls her husband in bed at night?" Carole had found her efforts at keeping a straight face impossible and had had to leave the room to regain her composure. It had been the beginning of a very happy friendship. No pretense, no fronts. But Carole was again reminded of the many meetings she would be expected to attend, and another tiny cloud popped up on her mental horizon.

Greetings and introductions continued as they made their way into the enormous ballroom that would accommodate their main meetings. The cavernous room was set up for the opening worship service. Carole's eyes swept the entire area, trying to take in everything at once. The place was alive with people finding their seats. Some of the faces were familiar, but Carole could recall only a few names. On the stage dignified men and women were taking their seats as the hidden organist began the prelude. A choir was banked around the back of the stage. As the low murmur of voices gradually began to fade, the rich true tones of a trumpet fanfare announced the beginning of the processional of banners and honored clergymen. Carole felt a tingle of anticipation. The choir led the convention congregation in the first hymn, and hundreds of voices blended in joyful praise to God. Carole felt herself responding with a heart full to overflowing.

The music touched her very soul; nothing moved her more deeply than the words of the hymns. She could feel Daniel's shoulder touching hers, and she felt herself absorbing his strength. This is the way she wanted to feel always. *Maybe this time,* she thought. *Maybe this time it will be different.* Hope rose inside her and swelled almost to the bursting point. She felt God's love and Daniel's love surrounding her, lifting her. There was nothing she couldn't handle. It *would* be different.

Too soon the service was over. But the euphoria of the worship service remained with her. She felt like a breathless bride, radiant and glowing.

It showed. Daniel leaned down and said softly, "I've never seen you like this, Carole. You're stunning!" And he swept her from group to group, proudly announcing their news.

They settled down for the opening address. The meetings were officially underway. All four sat together for this session and plowed through the convention workbook, trying to understand the official business of the church.

Carole was familiar with most of the current issues and voted accordingly. Occasionally she asked Daniel for advice. She noticed that Joyce voted much the same on most of the items.

"Enjoying yourself?" she asked her friend between speakers.

"I cannot tell a lie in the midst of all God's business." Joyce heaved a mighty sigh. "Yes and no. My mind is interested in almost everything, but my sitter is almost sat out. Is there always this much arguing at church conventions?"

"Honey, this one is mild compared to some I've been to," Carole said. She turned to Daniel. "We're going to go get some coffee and stand in the back for a while. Would you like some?"

"No, thanks." His attention was riveted on the speaker at one of the microphones.

"How can he listen so long without his ears falling off?" asked Joyce.

"Practice."

They threaded their way out to the table set with large silver urns filled with fresh coffee. Joyce's eyes widened. "Carole," she said in a low voice, "there's not a Styrofoam cup in the place. It's all china and silver spoons!"

"First-class all the way. Uh—oh! Come with me," she said tersely.

They moved behind a large pillar and sat at one of the small linen-covered tables.

"What's going on?" Joyce spooned in the packets of artificial sugar.

"Call me a coward, but I saw someone I don't particularly care to meet. At least not right away." Joyce waited. "It's just someone I had a run-in with years ago. Our misunderstanding was never resolved and I'm not ready to confront her yet."

"Someone from one of your churches?"

"Nope. A minister's wife. A veritable paragon of virtue." She drawled the words sarcastically. "You know the type. The perfect wife, mother, Christian, assistant pastor. You know, I never heard anyone ask her a question that she didn't have an answer for—usually documented with Scripture quotations." She looked at Joyce for the usual nod of approval. It was missing.

"I've never heard you knock another minister's wife before."

"You've never met this woman. Joyce, I guarantee you that five minutes with her and you'll know she's a phony."

"Carole!"

"Oh, she doesn't know that she's a phony. She thinks she's doing everything just right. She's following the footsteps laid down by whoever defines the pastor's wife's role in each church." She looked down into her coffee cup. "The saddest part of the whole story is that she doesn't know how she turns people off religion. She thinks living an unspotted life, one that is without any apparent problems in her view, is setting a good example for her congregation and friends." Carole uttered a small cry of pain.

"What's the matter?" cried Joyce, reaching for her hand.

"Oh, no! I'm going back into that circle again—the circle of the perfect sisterhood. I can't do it, Joyce. I just can't

100

sit around and listen to women like her again. There are too many of them in varying shades of perfection. I don't belong there." The panic in her eyes was real.

"Steady. You aren't going into that again. Even if you do, you have so much that you can teach those women."

"You can't teach the teachers," Carole said wryly.

"No, but you can be an example for them."

"Maybe if Jo and some of the others were there. But not alone."

"You don't know. There may be another mean little kid just like you, waiting for a cohort."

Carole laughed aloud. "All right. My immediate desire to pack and run off to Alaska has passed. But you know I'm right about some of those things."

"You love Daniel. That's the most important thing to remember."

"Correction. The most important thing to remember is that God has bailed me out every time I really needed Him. And am I going to need Him—very soon!" There wasn't much humor in the way she spoke those words. "Come on, Joyce, let's go."

Now there was one large cloud on her horizon. *How many clouds does it take to make a storm?* Carole wondered idly.

"I missed you. What took so long?" asked Daniel.

"Don't ask," replied Joyce with a grin.

The speakers droned on. Carole poked Joyce gently and motioned toward the ceiling.

It, too, was covered in velvet, but every few feet there was a domed area with a small crystal chandelier suspended from its center. There must have been more than a hundred of them across the ceiling of the ballroom.

"Lunch at last," said Daniel as he rose and stretched mightily. "Where would you ladies like to eat?" He smiled grandly at Mr. Miller. "Or is there somewhere special you would like to go, Mr. Miller?"

Well, there is a hamburger place that's recommended on the convention list," he said.

"That's fine with us, isn't it, girls?" Daniel's quick assent left no room for argument.

Carole reached for Daniel's hand as they started the walk to the restaurant across the street. They slowed their pace to put them behind Joyce and Mr. Miller.

"Quit staring at me," complained Carole.

"I see something in your face that's familiar to me, but I can't place the reason for it. Besides, it's a pretty face."

She held on to his hand more tightly. "I've seen a lot of people I know. It's been fun," she said a bit too brightly.

"Ah, now I recognize that look. Whom did you see who upset you so much?"

"It wasn't anyone special. Well, not really. Besides, you probably don't even know her. It doesn't matter."

"You forgot 'What difference does it make?' and 'I'd forgotten all about it' in your list of denials." He searched her face again. "Who was it, Carole?"

"Mrs. Perfect Christian Pastor's Wife."

Daniel laughed loudly. "I know her! And I can't believe you'd let her get to you." Seeing the sparks in her eyes, he retreated. "I see she did, though. Sorry."

"Oh, Daniel, I'm really mad at myself. How can these people make me feel so bad?" she fumed.

"Honey, haven't you figured that out yet?" Daniel's normally patient voice sounded a bit tired. "Just let go and be yourself, Carole. Quit watching people to see if they're watching you."

"I'm sorry to be such a burden to you while you're taking care of more important things," she said sarcastically.

Daniel refused to be drawn into her angry mood. "Just

wait until tonight and I'll show you important things," he said mysteriously.

"Daniel, this can't possibly be where we're supposed to be eating our lunch, is it?" Carole's eyes swept the peeling paint on the side of a clapboard building. A sign proclaimed: "Over Two Dozen Sold."

"Believe it or not this is one of the best places in the world to get a hamburger. It's part of a chain. Well, there *is* one more in Austin." His grin was a little sheepish.

With great trepidation Carole stepped over the wooden threshold into a large room filled with mismatched wooden tables and chairs. The floor was wood-planked and all types of antique-like pictures and furniture, tagged with sale prices, were arranged for browsing and buying.

The most heavenly smell of simmering meat and onions filled the air. Walking toward the order counter, they passed a table where a mannequin dressed as an Indian was permanently eating lunch. A sign reminded people not to touch "Old Joe." Carole and Joyce exchanged grins. The menu was simple enough: hamburgers.

Carole was enchanted. The place was obviously clean, and the clientele surprised her. They appeared to be younger men and women on their way up in the world who had discovered a delightful, old-fashioned place to eat. It began to occur to Carole that the atmosphere was carefully contrived to produce an effect of nostalgia.

Mr. Miller was pleased with the prices and became almost chatty during the delicious meal.

As they left the eating place, the foursome sensed that it would be a long afternoon, but seemed resigned to the prospect. Not everyone felt the responsibility of being a delegate as keenly, however, for the attendance was down considerably.

About ten minutes before the last item of business was

finished, Daniel leaned over to Carole. "I can't take even one more minute of this. I'm going up to the room. Want to come with me—to rest a while in the sitting room, of course," he added hastily.

"All right." Carole whispered an explanation to Joyce, disregarding Mr. Miller's frown.

They walked out in what Carole hoped was a nonchalant way, but she felt a thrill of excitement at the thought of being alone with Daniel. She had no intentions of anything improper happening, and she knew he wouldn't put her in an awkward situation. But the thoughts and feelings were there, nonetheless. By the time they paused in front of the door, her heart was racing.

Daniel closed the door behind them and immediately took Carole into his arms, kissing her soundly. "I've wanted to do that all day," he said against her mouth.

She clung to him, responding with warmth. "Isn't it nice that we want the same things?"

They walked to the couch and sat down close together. Daniel's strong fingers massaged the taut muscles at the back of her neck, then strayed to play with the tendrils of hair at her temple.

"You'd better stop that," she warned. "It could get you into trouble."

"Think so, huh?"

"Maybe more than you can handle."

"That sounds like a direct challenge. One that I may be prepared to accept," he said with a break in his voice.

The silence that followed crackled with tension, but neither one moved to put feelings into action.

"You know this is dangerous, don't you?" Carole finally asked.

"Yeah, old Miller might walk in at any moment."

"Is that what keeps you from making the first move?"

104

Daniel's face was a study in turmoil. "Yes—and no. I'd give anything if this were our honeymoon suite, Carole, but it isn't. I don't want to do anything that we would both regret later, that would damage my ministry or—more importantly—our witness. It wouldn't be worth the price we'd have to pay." His eyes were troubled.

"I'm glad you put it into words," she sighed. "Much the same thing has been running through my head since we came here. It will be hard, but I needed to know you feel that way, too. We'll be together and we'll get to know each other better. But we can prove to everyone that it's possible to be thrown into a tempting situation and yet not fall into the trap."

"I'd like to reconsider my stand. You make us sound so very wonderful, and I'm not wonderful at all. I just want the right things for us. Maybe the right thing, woman, is to drag you into one of those beautiful bedrooms." He reached for her playfully and she dodged his grasp.

In a mockingly lecherous voice, he intoned, "I may be a minister, but never forget for a moment that I'm also a man who's madly in love with a beautiful woman. Come to me, me pretty."

They collapsed, giggling like two teenagers, in a heap on the floor.

It was at that moment they heard a key scratching in the lock, and Joyce saying in a loud voice, "I know this is the right key, Mr. Miller. Just give me a minute to figure out which way it goes in the lock."

Quick as a wink they were on their feet, straightening hair and clothing, and sitting respectably in chairs far apart. They stood up as their suitemates entered the room.

"Is the session already over? We were just talking about how interesting the activities have been," Daniel said with a straight face. Carole nodded in agreement.

Mr. Miller glanced at the couple with suspicion, but since they were standing decorously across the room from each other, he seemed to dismiss any thought of impropriety and sank down heavily in one of the plush chairs.

"Well, we're back to what shall we do for dinner?" said Joyce. "I didn't mention it before, but I have an old school chum here in Dallas and I plan to go out to see her tonight. She's invited me for supper, too. I hope that will be all right with everyone." She smiled innocently at Carole.

"I hope you didn't make any plans for me," said Mr. Miller. "I told Pastor the only reason I accepted this job was that my mother lives here. I'm planning to visit her tonight. May stay the night, too. But I'll be here for the session tomorrow morning." Without further ado he entered his bedroom and began packing a few things.

Daniel and Joyce smiled a huge joint smile at Carole. "I see a conspiracy afoot here. Joyce, what will you really do?"

"I do have an old school chum in town. And we've been making plans to get together for months. Sorry, you two!" She grinned wickedly and walked toward the opposite bedroom.

Carole followed her inside and shut the door. "I'm not so sure this is a good idea, Joyce." Tiny specks of panic lit her eyes.

"I think it would make a lovely honeymoon suite."

"Joyce!" Carole was genuinely shocked. "I'm surprised that you would suggest such a thing."

"Don't get huffy with me, Carole. I honestly thought you might want to spend some time alone, that's all. After all, you are engaged and," she added "both of you are responsible Christian adults. But whatever you decide is your business—nobody else's."

Carole's voice tightened. "Don't think it hasn't crossed

my mind, but I don't like the idea of your reading it so easily."

Joyce came to Carole and put her arms around her. "Be happy, honey," she said. "The time is yours to spend as you see fit without someone looking over your shoulder." She snapped her small overnighter shut. "My taxi should be here any time now. See you tomorrow."

Carole and Daniel stood in the middle of the sitting room and watched Joyce and Mr. Miller go their separate ways. After they left, the silence was almost palpable, hanging between them like an invisible wall.

Daniel walked over to Carole and held her loosely in his arms. "This doesn't change anything we've talked about. Let's just enjoy this special time together. I've ordered a super dinner from room service. Then we can go out or spend the time here. You decide." He dropped a kiss on her nose.

"Oh, no, you don't. You're not going to leave all the decisions up to me. We're in this together."

"Shall we vote then?" His smile was irresistible.

"What are the options?"

"I'll leave that up to you, too." He laughed aloud as she aimed an ineffective punch at his arm. "Politics certainly do get you worked up, don't they?"

"Okay, let's look at this thing calmly. Dinner has already been ordered, so we know what we'll do for now." She crossed over to a chrome chair and plopped down. "The next question is what to do with the rest of the evening."

"Carole, you look so trapped, honey, even a little scared. Allow me to help you out of your quandary. We've decided where all the boundaries are. We're safe because we both know what we've agreed to. I, personally, would like to spend the time here. We can eat, talk, walk the halls, visit with other people in their rooms, or invite some of our friends here. Besides, my darling, you are perfectly safe with me. Just don't wear anything provocative."

Relief and then laughter flooded her face. "It's a deal! Oh, Daniel, I love you more than ever! You make everything so wonderfully simple."

The bear hug she gave him was interrupted by a knock at the door.

"Room service," called the young man pushing a dinner cart covered in white linen.

"Put it there by the window, please," instructed Daniel.

The waiter moved two chairs to the rolling table and opened the drapes to admit the late evening sun which illuminated the area with a golden glow.

Seating Carole, Daniel lit the candles with a flourish. "For later—when the sun goes down," he grinned.

Then taking his seat, Daniel reached for Carole's hand and they bowed their heads, thanking God for the food and for the miracle of the love they shared.

Uncovering the silver platters, they exclaimed over the tantalizing aromas coming from the beautifully garnished dishes.

"Daniel, have you really enjoyed the sessions so far?" Carole began the conversation.

"Most of them, yes. That really was a stirring worship service, wasn't it?" He took a big bite of the cold fruit compote.

"That's usually the part I like best. Perhaps it's the committee's way of getting the delegates psyched up for the drudgery to follow."

"Perhaps so. Confidentially, most of the business is cut and dried. Once in a while something really controversial comes up that requires serious discussion, but that's rare."

"Why do you bother to attend if you know the sessions are not going to be that interesting?" Carole was puzzled.

"Mainly because I need the spiritual renewal I find being with the other pastors, sharing the good things—and the bad. I need to know I'm not out there doing a job all by myself." He paused to slice the tender prime rib. "Sometimes I get some good ideas to try in my own parish from some of the other guys. And attending a worship service I didn't have to plan is refreshing and inspiring. Why? Are you sorry you volunteered to be a delegate?" he asked as he handed her the warm basket of buttery dinner rolls.

"Of course not," she protested, "but most of the business is pretty dull. Maybe I can't pick up on the undercurrents like you can. But I do understand what you mean about being recharged. I've picked up some pretty good ideas myself from some of the book displays." Shyly she added, "I think I'll enjoy the next convention more as your wife, rather than as a lay delegate."

Daniel's face softened in the candlelight. "Yes—as my wife."

"It seems a long time away, doesn't it?" she whispered. "Forever."

"Perhaps we could just stay here this evening and watch television. We still have some plans we need to finalize." Carole blushed, then struggled for composure. Daniel's presence was so disconcerting.

"I think that's a very practical suggestion, my dear," he nodded.

They completed the meal in relative silence, each concentrating carefully on the food. Vowing they would skip the next three meals, they carried their coffee cups to the plush couch. It was pleasant to sit together in the privacy of the luxurious room, sipping their coffee contentedly and sharing their dreams. Daniel's arm rested along the back of the sofa, lightly brushing Carole's shoulders. Her head nestled comfortably in the crook of his arm. She leaned back and sighed a sigh of pure contentment.

"What bliss—and what a wonderful way to live—even if it's only for a little while." Her eyes surveyed the elegant surroundings with a trace of covetousness.

"The home we're going to share isn't exactly a dump, you know," he chided. "You've done a fine job of making it a lovely, warm haven where we can be proud to welcome guests."

"Now, Daniel, don't tell me you don't enjoy the good life." She gave him a penetrating look.

"If you mean 'living rich,' I'd have to plead guilty—occasionally. But, Carole, this really isn't the 'good life.' To me, it feels—lonely," he said, searching for just the right word. He pulled her more tightly to him. "What we'll have together will be heaven." His voice faded away to a mere whisper.

Carole felt the passion rise between them. How she longed to end the waiting. *We are alone!* cried her heart. *But this is not right for you—or for Daniel!* counseled her head. And she hung suspended between her heart and her head, almost hoping that Daniel would dare to tip the scales one way or the other so she wouldn't have to decide.

Daniel pulled her even closer and wrapped his arms around her. His mouth teased a kiss from hers, then demanded a full response. She could do nothing but follow his lead, until she felt herself slipping toward that fine line she had been both dreading and hoping for. It would be so easy to go on—so hard to stop. *Stop!* the word resounded in her head. As she opened her mouth to say the word, Daniel pulled away from her. His face was flushed; his breathing erratic and labored. Carole was trembling.

"Well, on to Plan B," Daniel said shakily.

Carole smiled in spite of herself. "Good advice. I'll check my appearance before we face the rest of the world.

And you might want to wipe all that beautiful lipstick off. It isn't your color, anyway."

Shortly they met again in the sitting room. Daniel was pushing the dinner cart out into the hallway.

"Cleaning up after the scene of the crime?" Her words almost passed for a light remark.

"I'm just naturally neat." He inspected her carefully. "You don't look like you've been doing something you shouldn't."

"That's because I haven't. Come on, Daniel, it was a close call, and we shouldn't have put ourselves in such a tempting situation. We made it and I'm proud of us. Now let's get out of here."

At the elevator door, Daniel slipped his arm casually around her shoulders. Safely inside, away from onlookers, he said softly, "I love you, Carole."

"I love you, too." Just before they reached the ground floor, she added, "And tomorrow I'm going to buy some silver polish."

"What?"

"Silver polish. For my wonderful knight in shining armor." The doors slid open silently and they were soon in the lobby mingling with their friends, both old and new. Daniel was quick to share their glad tidings of their marriage with anyone who would listen.

The crowd began to thin out as the hour grew later. Carole and Daniel said their good-nights and went back to their suite.

"I enjoyed visiting with old friends tonight," offered Carole as they entered the sitting room.

"Me, too."

"But it's getting late, so I think I'll turn in," said Carole. A huge yawn underscored her remark.

"It's about that time."

She lifted her face to his. "It's so nice being able to kiss you good-night and know that you're close by."

He leaned down to brush her offered lips. I'm glad you came. Good-night, love."

"Sleep tight. See you early in the morning." Just before she closed her bedroom door, she glanced once more into the sitting room. Daniel was watching her. His look of intense longing was unmistakable. She blew him a kiss and quickly shut the door.

Carole showered and slipped into her gown, passing up the after-bath robe in favor of her own peignoir. She turned out the lights and opened the drapes, standing in the window to finish the nightly ritual of brushing her hair. The Dallas skyline was magnificent. It appeared as if a giant hand had carelessly scattered multicolored jewels over a black velvet robe. A long rope of pearls traced a wide highway over to her right. Garnets and rubies blinked at regular intervals along another, mixed with emeralds and canary yellow diamonds. Brilliant sapphires and white diamonds glittered at random. She stood high in her tower, feeling rich and pampered and blessed. *I wonder if he's watching the night, too,* she thought. It was of little comfort to remember that soon they would be able to share moments like these. Sighing, she turned down the covers and slipped into bed. Her eyes drifted again to the windows. A million shimmering stars softly lit the room and she concentrated on their beauty to block out the disturbing thought that Daniel was lying so near, yet so far away.

A pale orange-sherbet sun was just beginning to reach into the room when something awakened Carole. She struggled through her sleep to identify the sound. A crash? A groan? She moved groggily to her door, listening for the sound again. Hearing nothing, she opened the door a tiny

112

crack and peeped through. Mr. Miller was quietly turning the knob of Daniel's bedroom door. His actions seemed furtive, secretive.

*What in the world is he doing here at this hour?* she puzzled. And then it dawned on her. He had obviously come back to check on them. Stunned at the thought, she tried to think of another reason for his strange behavior. But nothing else occurred to her. He *is* checking on us. It was incredible! She wanted to yank the door open and scream at him. But she felt powerless to move, and for a moment she thought her searing anger had melted her to the floor. Mr. Miller slipped behind the door and out of sight, and she, too, noiselessly closed her door and staggered back to bed. She was shaking from the outrage surging through her body. And then a new thought struck her. In a few hours she would have to come face to face with Mr. Miller. There was simply no way to avoid their cozy quartet.

*There are two long days of the convention to go. And one more night,* she reminded herself. *What am I going to do?* She reached for the phone. *Daniel will know how to handle this.* But she took her hand away without dialing. *If I call him to come to my room now, it will be just as incriminating.* She decided to wait one more hour and then call him for an early breakfast. Maybe she could get out of the suite without seeing Mr. Miller.

When she did call Daniel, it was a relief just to hear his voice. She tried to make her own sound normal. "Daniel, can we get away to the coffee shop?"

"Sure. I can be ready in a little while. What's up?"

"We can discuss that over breakfast. Thirty minutes?"

"Yes, of course. Bye."

She did feel a little better. Her anger had cooled enough now to be manageable. She hurried through her morning routine and was just walking out of her room as Daniel opened his door. With relief she noted that Mr. Miller was nowhere to be seen.

"Good morning, my love. Did you sleep well? You look a bit tired."

"I'm fine," she said. "Let's hurry and get some coffee." Daniel's mouth was etched with tense lines.

The hallway was deserted, but Carole spoke in a low voice. "I am so mad I may get a migraine headache."

"I assume we are talking about Mr. Miller's early morning arrival," he said grimly.

"You bet we are." She considered a few choice remarks before settling for a more acceptable comment. "There is no way that I can be civil to that man for the next two days. What are we going to do?"

"My immediate reaction was to punch him in the mouth," he grinned weakly. "After he crawled into the other bed, I lay there awake. That is probably the most severe test of self-control I have ever endured. Even harder than leaving you last night." He put his arm around her protectively. The elevator doors opened for them and they stepped inside for the short ride to the coffee shop.

"Then you think he was checking on us, too?" At his affirmative nod, she continued. "I thought maybe I was just being paranoid."

"No, I think he thought he was going to find something. Disgusting, isn't it?" He shook his head in disbelief.

They interrupted their conversation long enough for the hostess to seat them at their table. Carole wasn't too upset to notice the beautiful crystal glassware and the heavy silver. It didn't look like a coffee shop. It was rather, a small jewel of a dining room, tucked away in the heart of the hotel. It lifted her spirits a little. They ordered quickly, and then continued with the matter uppermost on their minds.

"Well?" she prompted.

"I first thought I would confront him and call his hand. But he'd just deny it. I think the best way to handle this is to play his game. Somehow, we must face him and not let him ever know that we suspected what he was up to."

"A—I don't think that makes sense, and B—I can't," Carole protested.

"It *does* make good sense," he insisted. "By not appearing angry, we could defuse him. If we had nothing to hide, why would we be upset?"

"Your logic is wonderful! Now all I have to do is get rid of a ton of anger to carry it off."

"You wouldn't let a dirty old man get the best of you, would you?" A challenge gleamed from his eyes.

"Never! All right. I'll find a way." They finished their breakfast and started back up to the room. "You can go up there, Daniel, but I'm not ready. I'll just go on into the ballroom and wait for you and Joyce."

"By the way, Carole, I think it would be better not to mention this to Joyce. It wouldn't be fair for her to have to work her way through this on such short notice. If you feel you must tell her, wait until we get home."

"All right," she agreed, knowing it was sound advice.

During the next two days her anger diminished enough to carry out their plan. But she knew there would be others in the congregation wondering just what did go on in that beautiful hotel. And it stuck in her throat like a fish bone.

Doubts assailed her anew at her decision to marry Daniel, and only her great love for him kept her from taking the next plane to some far-away Pacific island.

## CHAPTER 8

CAROLE CLOSED THE LID of her suitcase with an authoritative snap. She surveyed her room and declared her packing finished. Then, adding a small traveling case to the luggage on the bed, she picked up her coffee cup. The door leading to the patio outside her bedroom was open and Carole strolled through it, sipping the steaming drink.

It was very early in the morning and the sun had just rimmed the tree-studded horizon. Spiderwebs of mist lay trapped close to the low places. It was going to be a day worthy of a wedding, she thought happily.

She smoothed her robe and stretched out on the lounger. Total calm rested quietly inside her steadily beating heart as she weighed the magnitude of this day. *Soon Daniel will live here with me*. She could almost visualize him moving around inside the house. A shaft of loneliness pierced her serenity. *I miss him. I want him here with me right now*.

As if he had anticipated her need, the phone rang at her elbow and she picked it up before it finished its first ring.

"Good morning!" said a cheerful voice. "How about a

date today, or do you already have plans?''

"Oh, I have plans all right! Are you ready to make a major change in your lifestyle?''

"Are you kidding? I've had my best suit on for an hour already. How about you?''

"Ah, not quite,'' she laughed, "but soon.''

He groaned dramatically. "From where I sit, it looks like a long time until the honeymoon. I still can't believe the church gave us two weeks at the beach as a present.''

"We'll be burned to a crisp by the time we get back.''

"Uh, I wasn't planning to spend that much time outside,'' he reminded her in a deliberately sultry voice.

"Daniel!'' she protested lightly.

"Lady, I've been very patient with you,'' he teased. "Now you get up and put on your best marrying dress. Today has *finally* come!'' The elation in his voice bubbled over the phone. "Eleven o'clock!''

"I'll be there,'' she said softly.

The appointed hour found Carole waiting calmly in the dressing room of the church, clad in a simple pale blue silk suit that accentuated her smokey blue eyes. When it was time to start the ceremony, she picked up her bouquet of deep red roses and walked from the room to the narthex of the church. Daniel was waiting for her there, to take her down the long aisle. They had decided to do it that way, for he said, "I don't want to wait for you any longer.''

She looked at him, misty-eyed with the love she felt for him, and choked down a sob of joy. He offered her his arm and they followed Joyce, gowned in pink, down the red-carpeted aisle. Carole heard only faintly the lovely strains of "Jesu, Joy of Man's Desiring.'' And though the church overflowed with well-wishers eager to be part of this memorable occasion, Carole had eyes only for the tall man at her side. Daniel, bathed in the brilliant-colored light emanating from the stained-glass windows, fairly glowed, and Carole thought her heart would stop before they finished their long walk to the altar.

Peter was waiting for them there, dressed in the black and white vestments of his office, a green stole around his neck. The candles on the altar burned brightly, symbolic of Christ's presence at their wedding. It was fitting that they walk together to present themselves before Him and to ask His blessing on their union, for together they would work in His vineyard.

In his text for the brief wedding sermon, Peter used a passage from the Gospel of Matthew in which the Lord promised, "Lo, I am with you alway, even unto the end of the world." In these words Carole felt that the Lord had spoken, assuring them that He would bless the fruit of their work and that He held their lives in the palm of His hand.

When they turned to face each other to repeat their vows, Carole spoke softly, love almost closing off the precious promises. Daniel's voice was husky with emotion, but the words rang clear and true.

"In the name of the Father, and the Son, and the Holy Spirit." Peter made the sign of the cross and said, "You may kiss your bride." It was a kiss that sealed their covenant, their future.

Carole was radiant as they walked back down the aisle to the triumphant chords of Purcell's "Trumpet Volentare." They stopped in the narthex and, caught up in the euphoria of the moment, Daniel drew her to him and gave her another soul-binding kiss. She saw tears of happiness in his eyes, and felt her own fill.

"I love you, Carole, my wife."

"And I, you, Daniel, my husband."

The people were coming from the church now with congratulations and wishes for great happiness, but it was apparent to all that this was an accomplished fact.

Then it was time to step into their future as man and wife. Joyce caught Carole's bouquet, and she gave a jubilant victory sign as the couple ran, laughing, to begin their married life.

"I guess all honeymoons must by necessity start in a car, but it is a nuisance," complained Daniel as he leaned toward Carole to give her one last kiss before going to their house to change clothes and pick up her luggage.

When they arrived at the door, Daniel swept her up and carried her over the threshold. "A pagan custom to keep you from stumbling through our married life, but I don't think I want to take chances now," he laughingly explained.

He carried her into the den and, without putting her down, kissed her once again. A husband's kiss for his wife. He steadied her as she regained her footing, then captured her in the circle of his arms. Carole was conscious only of Daniel's nearness and of the heavy perfume of the roses she still carried.

"Be careful of the roses," she whispered as he attempted to pull her closer.

"Would you let even a rose stand between us now?" he asked softly, his brown eyes heavy-lidded with love.

Carole slipped from his arms and walked a few paces from him, pulling a single flower from the bouquet and offering it to him. He followed, reaching for the red blossom, but she dropped it to the floor and pulled out another, stepping just out of his reach and leaving a trail of the fragrant flowers behind her as she led him down the hallway. There was but one long-stemmed bud remaining when she reached her bedroom, and she stood waiting for him to come to her. He took the last rose from between them and gave her a level look. This was right, and the time was

119

right. There would be no more waiting.

The landscape from the car window changed from gently rolling hills to flat land with coarse grass and a few Sago palm trees as they sped toward the island city of Galveston.

Galveston's main avenues were marked by giant oleander bushes striding down the middle of the streets, neatly dividing the lanes of traffic. They took the Sixty-First Street exit, and were soon driving along the seawall. The beach was a grayish-brown, and the muted colors extended far out into the many faces of the ocean. On the seawall, people were walking, skating, and riding three-wheeled adult bicycles. Carole noted with amusement that sprinkled among the deeply tanned bodies were those who had not been so prudent and showed evidence of the sun's burning rays. She made a mental note to pick up some suntan lotion at a little market she had spotted on the way.

Daniel and Carole were eager to reach the honeymoon cottage that was waiting for them on Jamaica Beach. It wasn't long and they were parked at the main office, talking to an attractive dark-haired woman named Janice who gave them their keys and directions to their temporary home.

Following the road paralleling the beach on a street colorfully named "Jolly Roger," they came to the last house on the block and, checking the number on their key, Daniel swung the car into the reserved space. The house itself was built as were all the other houses, on piers ten feet off the ground. It was perfectly square and entirely surrounded by a continuous deck. Climbing the stairs, the newlyweds stood looking out over the deep blue water, squinting at the reflection of the sun's rays bouncing off the white-capped water. Distant sounds of people at play floated to them across the sandy expanse.

"Oh, Daniel!" Carole exclaimed. "Our own watery Eden. It's perfect! Let's don't ever go back!"

"You may not find the winters so inviting," he commented. She made a wry face and hurried into the house.

The spacious living room was decorated in varying shades of blue. Couches in aquamarine and navy were built into two walls, while the kitchen bar dividing the room was in turquoise with matching stools from which to snack. To her left, Carole spied a pot-bellied stove with another couch nearby. The glass-jalousied windows were covered with Roman shades for privacy.

She walked through the kitchen, past a glass-topped wrought iron table and chairs and into the master bedroom beyond.

"Daniel!" she called. "Come in here! I don't believe this room—it's magnificent."

Here the decorator had chosen to create a mood of tropical splendor, using muted earth tones and the delicate colors of the rising sun. The bamboo furnishings were cast against a backdrop of cool creamy walls and the most luscious apricot carpeting Carole had ever seen. To accent the decor, there were baskets of palms and other lush foliage, transforming the room into a garden hideaway.

Daniel turned on the ceiling fan suspended over the king-sized bed and dropped down to enjoy the cooling breeze. Carole sat self-consciously beside his prone figure.

"I feel a little strange being here alone with you," she confessed. Hurrying on, she said, "I mean, it's all so new. At home it seemed natural. Now I feel, well, like you're forbidden fruit."

"Forbidden fruit is supposed to be the sweetest. Shall we find out?" He grinned and reached for her.

"Absolutely not," she insisted firmly. "Get yourself outside and bring in the rest of the luggage."

"There's always a snake in paradise," he grumbled good-naturedly.

After they were settled in, Daniel asked jokingly, "May I go out and play now? I've done all my work."

She laughed in spite of herself. "Only if you let me go, too. I want to look for sharks' teeth!"

She ran ahead with an unbridled exuberance that recalled the days of her childhood. Sitting down in an eddy filled with tiny white mussel shells, she explained, "I'm going to sift through these. This is the way I found my first shark's tooth when I was a little girl."

Sensing Carole's nostalgic mood, Daniel moved on down the beach, occasionally poking a likely looking object with his toe.

The water rushed in around Carole, scattering the shells and laying down an even more intricate pattern. As the water receded, the shells bumped together, making the tinkling sounds of a miniature windchime. A helicopter hovered high above like a huge dragonfly, checking the beach for distress signals, while seagulls circled and wheeled. The sand dunes were laced with coarse salt grass, and, arching overhead from shoreline to horizon, the sky was an impossible blue, blue. The moment, fusing the past and the present, was heartbreakingly beautiful.

"Hey!" called Daniel from a distance. "I think I've found one!" He ran back to her, holding the evidence in his palm, much like an errant school-boy bearing a bouquet of wildflowers.

Carole's heart turned over. "How wonderful, Daniel! That's the largest one I've seen. Here, I'll put it with these tiny ones I've found." She laid it tenderly with the others.

"Now, Mrs. Thornton, it's time for a swim." He pulled her to her feet and they ran, hand-in-hand, into the pounding surf. In minutes they were splashing and frolicking like children. Carole studied the handsome face of her new husband with unabashed joy. *Thank-you, Lord, for sending*

*Daniel into my life,* her prayer soared heavenward.

Later his strong body plowed through the water toward her. Reaching for her hand, he pulled her, unprotesting, to the hot sand. With no one in sight on the beach, he used the opportunity to claim her warm, salty mouth for his own.

"Hmm, you taste good. We could use a few French fries to go with that salt, though," he said, shattering her solemn reverie.

"Surely you don't expect me to cook on the first day of our honeymoon!" she said incredulously, raising herself to her elbows. "They have a wonderful invention here. It's called restaurants."

"I guess since you're making such a big deal out of this little trip, I may as well indulge you. I never dreamed you'd be so hard to domesticate." He thought of one more verbal arrow to sling, but found it hard to talk with gritty sand in his mouth. "Now that was really uncalled for," he said, lunging for her.

She was already several steps ahead of him, racing for the safety of the house. Her slim form fairly flew ahead of him, but the sand slowed her down a bit, and his long, strong legs made up for the advantage she had in her early flight. He caught her at the bottom of the steps leading up to their haven. Carole thought he was going to kiss her, but instead, he rubbed his sandy face all over hers in retaliation. She struggled unsuccessfully as he picked her up and carried her into the house.

Dinner at Gaido's satisfied their hunger, but the sea called to them again and soon they were walking the evening beach. The water nibbled at their toes as it struggled in and out.

Holding Daniel's hand, Carole felt safe and dared to speak of something that had been troubling her thoughts.

"Being married to you is even nicer than I had hoped," she began.

"Nice? Where is romantic, passionate, world-shaking?" he joked. Then sensing she had something important on her mind, "What is it, Carole?" he probed. "You've been thinking about something all through dinner."

"I see your radar is working." Her eyes searched the black water for late-night freighters on their way to the mouth of the Houston ship channel. "I've been thinking again what it will be like to be married to a minister."

"Here is the minister." His brow was furrowed as he waited for her to continue.

"You're not a minister here. You're a charming bride-groom, a new husband. You are not acting in your role as a minister."

"At least you recognize it as one of the roles I play—and not me." He frowned, "You aren't sorry already, are you?"

"No, no," she said swiftly. "I know you love me, and I truly do love you." She looked up at him in the moonlight trying to see his face clearly. "But I keep seeing the congregation all lumped together, I guess, as someone whose acceptance I must win."

"But you should be able to see that they are eager for you to be my wife. I've not heard one negative remark."

"What about Leigh?" she asked, hurt coloring her voice. "Why didn't she come to the wedding?"

"Now I think we're getting down to the real problem. I told you that she had to register for the fall semester of school."

The darkness obscured his face, but the words did have a ring of truth in them. Was there even the tiniest false note in his answer? Something inside her stirred uneasily. She followed her instincts, rather than the sound of his voice.

"She doesn't approve of me, does she?"

"I would rather say that she doesn't know you," he said kindly.

"I thought so."

He squeezed her hand a little more tightly and pulled her closer beside him. Then he stopped and turned to her so that the moonlight played on the strong planes of his face.

"I can't promise you that everyone is going to approve of you. I can't make my daughter give her blessing to our marriage. I can only love you and help you grow stronger. We'll face all obstacles that come our way together."

The days and nights passed in blissful succession, bringing renewed confidence and a new appreciation for the gentle man she had married. There was all the time in the world. Time for intimate discoveries, time for quiet moments of reflection and prayer on the deck overlooking the changeless sea, time for laughter and hilarity and fun, time for savoring the harmony of the universe that seemed to have been freshly created as a wedding gift.

"How can anyone with eyes to see deny the existence of God?" mused Carole late one afternoon as the sun sent flaming fingers of purple and pink splashing into the water.

"Hmmm, sometimes I think it's easier to believe in a remote Creator than in a personal, caring Father Who knows our humanness and loves us anyway," he replied. "I know I'll never stop beng grateful that he loved me enough to give me you, darling."

The answering glory in Carole's eyes rivaled the splendor of the sunset.

"Promise me something, Daniel."

"Anything my love."

"Promise me that if it gets bad back there, we can come here to find ourselves again."

He caught her hand and dropped a kiss in the palm.

And then it was time for one last stroll along the beach.

"It's so beautiful here," said Carole, squeezing Daniel's hand. "I never get tired of the sound of the waves coming in. Have you noticed how loud the surf is when there is nothing to distract you?"

He cocked his head and listened intently. "It's a constant roar, isn't it?" His eyes traced the watery path of light reflected from the sinking sun.

There was no music on that deserted beach—only the sounds of the surf and the cry of an occasional solitary gull stepping gracefully to the water's edge, moving to some primal rhythm. But Carole could hear the music in her soul, echoing the refrain, *With this man I can be happy. With this man I can be safe.*

Breathing deeply of the salt air, Carole felt the last of her tension and apprehension drain away. Leaning back into the circle of Daniel's arms, she said softly, "I'm ready now—to go home."

## CHAPTER 9

THE ENTIRE CONGREGATION turned out for the old-fashioned pounding held in the fellowship hall the week after Carole and Daniel returned from their honeymoon. There were pounds of all the staple items and a wide variety of canned goods to fill their pantry to overflowing. Carole was touched by this outpouring of love from the people. She had never felt so happy in her life.

Daniel stood beside her, surveying the huge pile of gifts and enjoying the homemade ice cream and cake. His eyes were shining as he said, "What a wonderful night. The people have been more than generous." A little more softly he added, "Looks like you've won their hearts completely." Carole's answer was a dazzling smile.

A strapping teenager with a group of assorted friends in tow came over and offered shyly, "Pastor, all us guys in the youth group would be glad to load this stuff in my pickup truck and take it to your house for you."

"That would be terrific! We surely would appreciate the help." He shook the boys' hands.

Right behind the boys came a rather portly lady. "Oh, Pastor, I'm just dying to tell both of you how happy we are for you." Her face and both her chins were wreathed in smiles as she continued, "And, Mrs. Thornton, we of the morning Ladies' Group are sure hoping you'll be at our next meeting. We're looking forward to having you as one of our new members." Carole opened her mouth to reply, but the lady rushed on, "Now, you don't have to thank me, dear. We'll just be looking for you on the first Tuesday of each month. You'd make a perfect program chairman for us, you being the pastor's wife and all. Well, I mean, since the pastor doesn't often come to our meetings," she cut her eyes up to the dignified figure of her pastor, "you'd make a lovely replacement for him." She smiled sweetly and moved away in a cloud of chatter to greet other guests standing in groups talking and laughing.

Carole laughed. "I think I've just been drafted."

"You'll enjoy getting to know that group of ladies. They're the salt of the earth."

"What I want to know is, how do *you* manage not to attend their meetings?"

"Practice, my dear, practice. I know how to say no, and still not wound them too deeply—a trick, I might add, that you will have to learn soon."

"I'm enjoying all this fuss. Makes me feel important. Besides, I can take care of myself. I've done it before, you know," she retorted.

"We'll see. Here comes the president of the other ladies' group—the *afternoon* group."

Daniel's smile was paternal, Carole thought, as they listened to virtually the same sales pitch. She was able to get only a word or two in. As the president of the afternoon group walked away, Daniel's only comment was: "Ah, at least you got to say yes to this one."

"But I *wanted* to belong to this one. I know most of the ladies," she protested. "And at least I'm not slated to be the new program chairman," she defended stoutly.

"Perhaps being the telephone committee chairman will be less time-consuming," he suggested helpfully.

"Let me get some more ice cream to take the place of the foot in your mouth, dear," she said as she walked away with his bowl. She spotted her good friend, Joyce, washing dishes in the kitchen and made a beeline for her.

"Help! I've gotten myself into a terrible predicament!"

"Already? You've only been back a week." She wiped her hands and handed Carole a dishtowel. "Here, dry these while I try to straighten out your life for you. Now, what's the problem?"

"Sally just asked me to join the afternoon ladies' group."

"That's great. I've been trying to get you to come for ages."

"That was right after Prudence informed me that I was going to make a wonderful program chairman for the *morning* group!"

"Her name really ought to be Imprudence. What did you tell her?"

"I never did get a word in edgewise, but it's all settled as far as she's concerned."

Joyce gazed into a large glass bowl she was washing and said, "I see the answer coming in on my crystal ball clearly." She passed her hand over the bowl and said in a bad imitation of a gypsy reader, "It says, 'Say no, or knuckle under.' There, that was very simple. Anything else I can do for you?" She grinned broadly at Carole's grimace.

They watched Daniel making his way over to them, and Carole asked wryly, "Are you sure you're not related to him?"

"We're just about ready to start wrapping things up," he

called. "Are you ready, Carole? Hi, Joyce. The ice cream was delicious. Did you bring some?"

"Hi! No, not this time. I brought the German chocolate cake."

"I had some of that, too. Why don't you give Carole your recipe," he suggested smoothly. "We'll see you later, Joyce. And thanks again for everything."

"My pleasure. Call you tomorrow, Carole, to see if you need any more help."

Carole just shook her head as she headed out the door.

Walking to the car, Carole suddenly remembered something.

"Hey, in all the excitement I haven't had time to ask you. Where was Tillie tonight?"

"Without her teletype running the underground gossip system, I guess you haven't heard. It seems Tillie is in traction at our local hospital. She sprained her back rather badly learning to waterski."

"Waterski!" Carole hooted. "What a sight that must have been! I can just see that red hair blowing in the wind." Frowning, she asked, "Will she be there long?"

"I heard a nurse muttering something about 'Either she gets out soon, or we're going to wire her jaws together!'" They looked at each other knowingly.

"We really need to go to see her, Daniel." Carole's voice softened with concern.


By the next afternoon Carole had put away all the gifts of food to her satisfaction and was just starting supper when Daniel came home. "Hello, did you have a good day at the office, dear?"

"Well, the Wilsons are getting a divorce, Mrs. Gerhardt is in the hospital again, and Mr. Wilcott says he's going to find a new church home if I don't quit using what he calls 'jokes' in my sermons." His smiling face was in stark contrast to the gravity of his news.

"Is that all? Nothing exciting?" Even in the short time they had been married, she had found reason to be amazed at his resilience.

"What's for supper?" He opened the lid of one of the steaming pans on the stove. "Mmmm. Chicken-fried steak. One of my all-time favorites." He kissed the back of her neck as she finished mashing the potatoes. "You're a fine cook. Sure glad I married you." His eyes grew serious. "And not just becaue of your cooking. You're a wonderful wife, Carole. And I'm hungry as a bear! Need any help in here?"

"Nope. Dinner is almost ready. You just sit down and tell me about your day. Did Mr. Wilcott really mean what he said about leaving?"

"It's hard to tell. However, I have no intention of being blackmailed into anything. When we've lost some of our best people in the past, the Lord has always been gracious enough to send someone to help fill the big hole they left behind. You have to consider the source. Mr. Wilcott is a dour man—no joy in his Christianity. I suppose his concept of worship is total solemnity. There are too many passages in the Bible about dancing and singing for me to believe that the only way to worship the Lord is with a sober face. To me, joy is what it's all about. I think I'll just let the Lord take care of things, especially since I know I don't have the power to change Mr. Wilcott."

"Will you be able to do anything to help the Wilsons?"

"I may be able to get them to talk to each other. It's a funny thing. I've noticed that often, when either a husband or wife stops coming to church, I later find out there's trouble at home. Sometimes people are ashamed to come to their pastor and admit they're having problems. They seem

131

to feel that a 'good' Christian should never have those problems in the first place."

"It's a little like waiting to go to the doctor until your cancer is terminal, isn't it?" she said.

"Exactly. And we ministers aren't entirely blameless. Most ministers do seem to hide the fact that they don't always bat a thousand in domestic matters. Maybe they're ashamed, too. It's time to show that we're human beings and climb down off our pedestals."

As Carole put the food on the table, the phone rang. "Hello," she made a face at the intrusive instrument. "Yes, how are you? Fine." She wrinkled her brow in a look of discomfort. "Well, yes, I suppose I could this once. It's been a while since I taught Sunday school for kids that age. Of course. . . . No, I've never been a teacher. I am, or was, the vice president at the bank, handling loans and that sort of thing. . . . No, I have a degree in business and financing. . . . And you'll bring the material over to me? . . . Oh, at the church. All right. Yes. Good-by." She replaced the phone and sat down at the table. "No need to tell you what that's all about. I don't mind filling in for her this time. I just hope she doesn't make a habit of calling me." She heard a chuckle coming from the other side of the table. "If you say one word. . . ," she warned.

"Just six. Welcome to the Sunday school program."

"I want to do what I can to help," she said a bit stiffly. "And I do have the time now. Besides, this will be a good way to get to know some of the children better. I think I'd like to give it a try. On a part-time basis, of course."

"Of course. I'm sure you'll enjoy it. Do you have anything planned for tonight? I'm going to call on a young couple who just moved to town. Should be a very enjoyable visit. Maybe you'd like to come with me?"

Her face lit up. "Yes, I'd love to come. As I recall, that's one of the best parts of being married to a minister."

"For me, too. Especially when it's just a social call. I'll help you clean up after supper so we can go early . . . I like watching you move around in our kitchen, Carole."

When Daniel covered her hand with his own, she could feel the love in his touch. "We don't have to stay out late, do we?" she asked. "I'd like a little time with you all by myself."

"No, we won't stay out late—now that I have someone to come home to."

Sunday morning they were up earlier than usual. It would be Daniel's first Sunday back in the pulpit since their marriage. Carole was exhilarated.

Daniel came out of the shower neatly groomed, lacking only his clerical shirt, which was neatly pressed and hanging in his closet.

"Are you ready for your egg?" She hurried to the stove to slip in the pot roast and vegetables she was preparing for their noontime meal.

"No, I'll just have bacon and toast. I never eat eggs on Sunday. Oh, and fruit juice. You look pretty this morning. However, I guess you're planning to wear a dress instead of that peignoir. Too bad! It could have livened up things considerably."

"You're trying to get me in trouble on my first official day as the pastor's wife. Shame on you." He didn't look shamed at all. In fact, he positively glowed with joy.

"All ready for your Sunday school lesson?"

"Yes, all ready, and a little nervous, too." She helped herself to a glass of orange juice.

"Are you going to talk to Prudence about not joining her ladies' group today?"

The question caught her off guard and she hesitated, her

juice glass poised in midair. "I hadn't thought about it. I suppose I should."

"Would you like me to speak to her?" he asked kindly.

"Certainly not! I can get myself out of this. But thanks for offering," she hastily added. "I'm just going to tell her, well, never mind, I'll know what to say when the time comes."

"I'm sure the Lord will give you just the right words. Say, we'd better hurry along, or we'll be late for our debut."

"All I have to do is slip on my dress. I bought a new one just for today."

In a matter of minutes they were on their way to the church. Arriving so early seemed strange to Carole. One of the ladies was still arranging the candles on the altar and putting out the flowers for the service. The organist was getting in a few more minutes of practice. And an usher was folding the bulletins.

"I'll come to your study just before church starts, Daniel."

"See you later, love. Good luck with your class."

It wasn't good luck that Carole needed during her class. It was patience. The children were small and their attention span, short. After the simple lesson, she managed to find things to keep them busy until their parents finally came to get them at the end of the long hour. Satisfied that she had done a creditable job on such short notice, she walked cheerfully over to Daniel's study in the church.

"Do you need any help vesting?" she asked him.

"Just be sure I don't have anything caught up in the back. I once went out with a coat hanger hanging from the back of my robe. I just couldn't figure out what all the gaiety was during that service. For a while I thought I had them in the palm of my hand."

She laughed as she adjusted his vestments carefully. "You're fine today." Kissing him sweetly on the cheek, she admonished, "Don't preach too long, or we'll have a burned pot roast for lunch."

*"Et tu, Brute?"* But his grin didn't look as if he had been truly betrayed.

She walked outside and around to the front of the church, greeting people and thanking them for the things they had brought to the pounding. She found what she considered to be her usual pew in the crowded church and bowed her head for a brief prayer. The prelude began and the last of the stragglers hurried to their pews. Daniel came in and walked to the altar to begin the service.

He spotted her during the first hymn and nodded his head to her slightly in greeting. It made her feel warm inside that he had searched her out, and special that he had chosen her above all others to be his wife.

When he stepped into the pulpit to begin his sermon, she was distracted by the memory of what he had eaten for breakfast that morning and even what he was wearing under all those ecclesiastical vestments. She fought down the urge to giggle.

As he began a humorous story, she had to resist the temptation to look around for Mr. Wilcott. Then as Daniel began the prayers for the day, he included one for harmony and understanding between husbands and wives, and she wondered if either of the Wilsons were present. *I wish I hadn't known quite so much,* she thought. She closed her eyes tightly and concentrated on the prayers Daniel was praying. During the offering she spotted Prudence, and prayed heartily for the right words to tell her that the morning ladies' group was going to be short one program chairman.

Walking up the aisle after the service, Carole saw the pretty Mrs. Wilson alone, and wondered if she should say something comforting to her. It suddenly struck her that the Wilsons' divorce might not yet be public knowledge. If she said anything, it might break the confidentiality of Daniel's position. She chose, instead, to greet Mrs. Wilson with a friendly smile and handshake.

She made it all the way to the door before Prudence caught up with her.

"I'm glad to see you this morning. I've been thinking of some things you might want to use for your programs this coming year," said the stout Mrs. Smithington, her chins wagging jovially.

"Prudence, you're just the person I need to see. Come on over here where we can visit a bit." She led the unsuspecting lady to the side, out of the flow of traffic. "I'm so grateful you asked me to join your group," she began, while Mrs. Smithington nodded in assent. "But I find that I won't be able to come on a regular basis. You see both groups want me to join and there's just no way I can do justice to them both."

Prudence's face had taken on a purplish hue. "But you aren't working now. You have plenty of time," she said with more than a hint of indignation.

"Well, not really. I find myself getting involved in quite a few activities. I do promise to come every other month, though. And I'll be glad to help in any way I can," she added in a conciliatory tone.

"I suppose that's better than nothing," conceded Prudence. She put on her stiff upper lip and launched on. "Our first meeting is Tuesday morning at nine-thirty sharp. You will come, won't you?"

Carole just didn't have the heart to say no. "Of course. See you then." She patted Prudence's shoulder and the matronly Mrs. Smithington walked away in search of more new members. *I hope I handled that the right way,* she thought to herself. *But only time will tell.*

When the organist appeared, Carole took the opportunity to tell her how much she had enjoyed the music.

"Thank-you, Mrs. Thornton. I understand that you play, too."

Carole sensed the sand slipping from beneath her feet. "Oh, some," she shrugged. "I have played in the past, but only in emergencies."

"If I ever have an emergency, would you play for me? I'm the only organist at the present, and I could surely use the help," she said hopefully.

"Well, I—I guess I could, if it were a real emergency and I knew the hymns early enough," she stammered.

"That's easy. Your husband chooses the hymns. You should be able to have them as early as you like," she laughed. "Thanks a lot. Bye, now."

"Don't worry, Carole, I'll see that you have plenty of time to practice those hymns," said her husband's voice behind her.

She turned around slowly and stood her ground, "Only in an emergency," she repeated, firmly.

"That emergency will be coming up in about a month. She has to play for her sister's wedding in Amarillo. On a Saturday night. Come on, darling. Let's go home and take out that pot roast before it gets too brown." He led her away to their waiting car.

The roast wasn't too brown, and after they had eaten, they both gratefully crawled into bed for a good afternoon nap.

"You know, Daniel, I used to go to church, carrying my own burdens and joys. Now I spend a lot of time thinking about the problems of other people. I can't decide if that's good or bad."

"I'd say it depends on whether or not you spend that time

worrying, or praying and trying to do something constructive. Worrying only wears you out. On the other hand, praying and trying to find an answer can build spiritual muscles. One thing I have learned—I can't solve other people's problems. I can only help people discover their options. Ultimately, they must make their own decisions.''

"Sounds like good advice. However, I don't believe you practiced that with me," she said. He looked quizzically at her. "You certainly didn't give me any options, other than to marry you."

He moved closer to her. "I had already done the praying ahead of time. I had chosen my option. All I needed was to convince you to follow it. Think of all the worry and praying I saved you!" She sighed contentedly and snuggled down closer to him. "You know it was the right decision for both of us, don't you?" he said as he nuzzled her forehead with his lips.

"Yes, darling—for both of us."

Two days later Carole was sitting in the fellowship hall, surrounded by the ladies of the morning group. Their greetings had been genuinely cordial. Silence finally settled over the group as Prudence called the meeting to order and asked the chaplain of the group to lead them in prayer.

This accomplished, she turned to welcome visitors and new members to the meeting.

"We are pleased and honored to have our pastor's wife with us today. She will be one of our new members. At least she will be a part-time member. Murmurs were heard around the room at this new designation. "What I mean is that she will be attending our meetings every other month." All eyes were now on Carole, and she felt her cheeks redden slightly. "Welcome to our group, Mrs. Thornton."

All she could think to say was, "Call me Carole,

please.'' She wished Prudence had given her a chance to explain to the group about her strange membership. Maybe she would get a chance later on. The meeting droned on, and Carole tried to listen carefully to get an idea of the scope of their activities. As Daniel had said, they were the salt of the earth. They performed, behind the scenes, all the unglamorous tasks that make a church run smoothly. There was nothing intellectually stimulating here, but Carole was eager to help where she could. She volunteered to help clean the church after a forthcoming wedding, and to bring two cakes for next week's bake sale. She thoroughly enjoyed the social part of the meeting, for it gave her an opportunity to get better acquainted with some of the ladies, especially Daniel's secretary, Janet Rogers. Soon she was hurrying home like the rest of them to prepare lunch for her husband.

Daniel was home ahead of her, putting out things for a quick sandwich.

''I'm sorry I'm late, darling. I was talking with some of the women and lost track of the time.'' She helped him put the finishing touches on their lunch.

''How was it?''

''Quite nice. That's a busy bunch. I could spend all my time with their activities alone. How do they do all the things they do?''

''Most women belong to just one or two organizations,'' he said pointedly.

''So do I.''

''I'm just reminding you not to get yourself overscheduled. This is not a new role for you.''

''You're trying to protect me from myself, and I love you for it, but let me do these things.'' Her eyes were pleading.

''Just know for whom you're doing them.''

She looked at him, startled. ''I know,'' she said softly.

They sat down to eat and Daniel asked, ''Can we have

dinner a little early tonight? This is my night to make hospital calls."

"Yes, of course. Are you going to see Tillie?"

"Wouldn't miss it. Would you like to go along?"

Delightedly she consented, and then added, "Poor Tillie."

"I wouldn't worry about Tillie. She can take care of herself. We may not like the way she goes about it, but Tillie provides us with a constant reminder that though we may not like everybody we meet, we do have to love them."

"Can you honestly do that, Daniel? Love everybody, I mean? I get so annoyed at some of the stupid things our people do, especially if it's hurtful and unnecessary."

"Not always," he confessed. "If you want perfection, you'll have to wait for heaven. Your husband isn't perfect." He laughed, then grew serious. "Perhaps it would help if you viewed some people as spiritual infants, then you could overlook some of their foibles."

"You're such a rock."

He looked earnestly into her eyes. "Even rocks can be broken, you know. Sometimes they are worn away by water, eroded by time. I'm not as strong as you perceive me to be, though it *is* flattering to be thought of as a tower of strength." His voice took on a warning note. "Be careful that you see the man in me, Carole. Sometimes I have the uncomfortable feeling that your love has covered too many of my sins."

She rose and went around to his side of the table. Kneeling beside him, she stroked his face lightly with her fingertips.

"Daniel, I do love you—perhaps too much—but I know you'll never do anything to hurt me. I will be careful not to push you into sainthood yet, but there is so much good in

140

you, so much more than in most people. You're so kind and loving, and you give of yourself to everyone. Sometimes it's hard for me to remember your faults." Rising, she added, 'Although you did forget the trash again last night."

His chuckle was muffled in her soft form. He raised his lips to the spot above the buttons on her blouse where her breasts rounded out slightly and kissed its sweetness. "I told you I wasn't perfect."

"Don't you have an appointment at one o'clock? If you do, you'd better get your mind on your business."

"Only my great strength allows me to remember that my pastoral duties call." His smile was broad and his eyes knowing. They both knew Daniel could reschedule his afternoon appointments. Neither moved, unwilling to make the choice. The ringing of the phone decided for them. Daniel sighed and stood to answer it.

"Hello, yes, Bea. You were able to get him to speak for the workshop? Good. What was that date again? Okay. No, we'll have him stay here with us. You're a very efficient lady. Thank-you for a job well done. Yes, good-by." He hung up the phone and, turning to Carole, said, "All right, that's all lined up."

"Are we going to have company?"

"Yes, on the twenty-seventh. Dr. Heckman will be the guest speaker for our fall workshop."

"I'm glad he's coming. I remember Dr. Heckman. I think I'll bake some blueberry muffins for his breakfast, since I know he loves them."

"I love them, too. Do I have to wait until the twenty-seventh?"

"No, love, I'll bake some in celebration of your great strength. Unless you'd rather I cut your hair tonight." She smiled a crooked smile.

"Later, Delilah, after we get back from the hospital."

The hospital door swished open quietly as Daniel and Carole entered Tillie's room. She was trussed up in straps, looking miserable, but her face brightened when she saw them.

"Pastor! And Carole, too. You have no idea what a terrible experience I've been through. And it's so lonely here." Her eyes misted with tears, and Carole was moved, for Tillie's misery was obvious.

"Hello, Tillie," said Daniel. "How are you feeling, aside from being lonely?"

"Miserable, just miserable. Those nurses don't come when I ring for them, my back hurts, my neck hurts, my jaw hurts, the food is terrible, and nobody has come to see me but you."

"Have the doctors said when you can go home?" asked Carole, unsuspectingly unleashing another diatribe from Tillie.

"And that's another thing. The doctor just gives me the runaround when I try to pin him down about when I can leave." Her baleful expression turned into a pout.

"Would you like me to speak to him for you?" offered Daniel.

"Oh, would you?" Relief flooded her face. "Maybe he'd talk to somebody *important*."

"I'm not sure how important I am, but I'll be glad to speak for you." He patted Tillie on the shoulder, offered a brief prayer for her comfort, and concluded his visit. "I'll talk to him in the morning and get right back to you. Good night, Tillie."

As they walked back down the long polished halls to see Mrs. Gerhardt, Carole commented, "Maybe some of the ladies could get things ready for her homecoming. A hot meal and a clean house would be a start."

"Is that one of the projects you ladies have taken on?"

"No, but surely they would be eager to help."

"Tell me, how many activities have you already scheduled?"

"There's a bake sale next Sunday and the cleaning and serving for the Foss wedding. That's all."

She pointedly ignored the implication of his question, choosing instead to end their conversation as they reached Mrs. Gerhardt's door.

## CHAPTER 10

THE NEXT AFTERNOON Carole decided to give the living room a thorough cleaning. She girded herself for her battle with dirt by pulling her hair into a ponytail and slipping into a pair of old jeans previously used for a painting project.

She pulled down the drapes and put half of them in the dryer for a good dusting. Then she moved all the furniture out from the walls to clean the baseboards and vacuum the carpet. She was in the middle of her task when the doorbell rang.

"No," she wailed, "not company now!" She looked at the utter chaos around her, but hurried to answer the insistent bell. The last person in the world Carole wanted to see was standing on the front porch. This woman had no peers when it came to housekeeping, and she was surreptitiously called "Mrs. Clean" by the other ladies of the church. She seemed more than a little startled at Carole's appearance.

"Hello, Mrs. Thornton! I just dropped by to bring you a little something for dessert."

Carole swallowed her pride and greeted her unwelcome

visitor. "Why, Mrs. Charles, won't you come in? I was just getting some early fall cleaning done. Please excuse the mess." She took the cake from the portly lady.

Mrs. Charles stepped into the entry hall like a cat treading on water and raised disapproving eyebrows when she saw the disorderly room. Stepping gingerly around the furniture that was spilling out into the hallway, she walked on to the den where there was less clutter. Carole stifled a grin, for Mrs. Charles reminded her of Goldilocks in the story of "The Three Bears" as she tried to decide in which chair to sit. *That one is probably too soft for her,* thought Carole as Mrs. Charles finally landed.

"Would you care for some coffee or tea? It won't take me a minute to make either."

"Yes, iced tea would be fine." Her eyes roamed the room, taking in everything. "You have a nice home. It isn't very large, though, is it?"

"With just the two of us, we don't need a lot of room," replied Carole as she walked to the kitchen, praying things were in order there, for Mrs. Charles had risen and was close on her heels.

"This is pleasant." Her eyes were now taking rapid inventory of the kitchen.

"Thank-you. Would you rather sit in here to have our tea?"

"That will be fine." Mrs. Charles settled herself into the chair and smoothed down the tablecloth in front of her.

Carole, feeling that she had already failed the test, stifled her anger and determined to be a gracious hostess. Choosing two glasses from a wedding gift set, she filled them with cubes of ice, poured the amber liquid that had been steeping in the teapot, and garnished them with sprigs of mint.

"My daughter has a set of those. They're pretty to be so inexpensive."

"Yes, we're enjoying them," said Carole, attempting valiantly to overlook the innuendo.

"Tell me, dear, what do you do with all the time you have since you quit your little job at the bank?"

Carole refilled her glass, stalling for time to suppress her indignation. "I'm finding myself quite busy with all my activities at the church. In fact," she added unwaveringly, "being a pastor's wife seems to be more time-consuming than my job as vice president of the bank ever was."

"Well, I know you're glad to finally have a husband and settle down again."

Carole didn't dignify that remark with a response, but was even more surprised by Mrs. Charles's next statement.

"I'd love to see your house, if you don't mind."

It was on the tip of Carole's tongue to deny the impudent request, but she consented rather than to appear unfriendly or ashamed of her home. "Of course." Carole dutifully gave her a tour of the rooms.

As soon as she had seen the house, Mrs. Charles announced, "Oh, my! It's getting late. I must go."

Carole walked her to the door. "Thank you for the cake," she said politely.

"You're welcome. Just be sure to return the plate, dear."

Carole closed the door with a sigh. "Patience, child, patience," she muttered under her breath. She sat back down at the kitchen table and tried to sort out her feelings. She was angry with herself for taking part in such a ridiculous charade, and yet she honestly didn't know what else she could have done. *All my instincts tell me I should just have asked her to come back another day,* she thought. *Why was I compelled to let her come in here and run over me like that?* Finding no answer, she fell back on her usual way of dealing with anger; she cleaned the entire house as if it had never been cleaned before.

146

When Daniel came home for supper, he found an exhausted Carole and a sparkling clean home. He eyed the cake on the kitchen cabinet and remarked, "You've had a visit from Mrs. Charles."

"How did you know?"

"She always brought me that cake when she wanted to check up on me. I used to scatter around a few newspapers when I saw her coming—just to keep things from being too tidy."

"You're a brave man under fire."

"Nope. I just like watching her eyebrows going up and down."

Carole burst into relieved laughter. "Daniel Thornton, I love you!"

"Because I'm messy?"

"No, because you always know how to put things in perspective."

"She was just curious about how we live. There are people like her everywhere, wanting to peek into other people's lives. It's just another form of voyeurism, but more socially acceptable."

"Then let's have an open house and give the entire congregation a chance to satisfy their curiosity." Her eyes shone with excitement as she contemplated the prospect of a party. "Christmas would be a good time, and it would give me a chance to repay some of our social debts."

"Sounds good to me. I love entertaining. In fact, there are some special people I'd like to invite over before then, Carole. Could we ask the Rogers for supper sometime soon?"

"Your secretary and her husband?"

"Yes, you've met them, but I'd like for you to get to know them better." Daniel pulled out his little red calendar book and consulted the heavily marked month. "This Friday would be good for me. About seven o'clock?"

Carole was putting their supper on the table. "Fine. I'll ask them tonight. We'd better hurry, though, or we're going to be late for church."

As Carole took her place in her usual pew, she nodded a friendly greeting to friends and acquaintances. She bowed her head for a brief prayer and settled back to enjoy the quiet background music. As her mind wandered over a variety of subjects, it began to focus on a growing revelation. *I've known these people for quite a while yet, I feel so differently about them now that I'm married to Daniel,* she mused. *And they treat me differently, too. Once I was a rather faceless individual. Now I feel so spotlighted.* She shifted uncomfortably in her seat. *Why is everything so different? I'm the same person I was before I married Daniel. But people seem to expect so much more from me, as though I had risen to some sanctified plane.* Her thoughts were interrupted by the doctor's wife sitting next to her.

"Mrs. Thornton," she whispered, "the ladies of the altar guild would be so pleased if you would join us. By tradition, the pastor's wife always acts as a guide for our activities. I know you're probably very busy, but we really need you in our organization." Her smile was beatific.

Carole began her protest, "But I know nothing about the altar guild. . . ."

The doctor's wife cut her off, "Oh, don't be so modest, my dear. You'd make an excellent leader. We'll see you next Monday night." The woman looked radiant now that her mission was accomplished, and she sighed a happy sigh as the service began.

Outwardly Carole smiled. Inwardly she fumed at the aggressiveness of the lady sitting beside her. The entire service was lost to her as her anger mounted. It was all she could do to be civil after the service, but she played her part well and no one suspected that she was furious.

Daniel knew her state of mind as soon as he saw her, but waited until they were alone to question her. "You look like a capped volcano. What happened?"

"That woman," sputtered Carole. "That woman had the nerve to conscript me into the altar guild. I tried to tell her no, but she didn't hear a thing I said. What am I going to do?" Her eyes were flashing dangerous blue sparks.

"What are your choices?" asked Daniel reasonably.

Carole stopped her angry pacing and glared at him. "I can go, or I can refuse to go," she shot back.

"Which one are you going to do?"

"I'm going to tell her absolutely no," she said flatly. She clenched her jaws tightly, then sighed a defeated sigh. "But she'll be mad, because 'the pastor's wife always acts as a guide for our activities'."

"And you don't want her mad at you?"

"I don't want to cause any trouble in the church, and you know as well as I do this could start something."

"It's all right to have conflicts within a church. It just takes a bit of skillful negotiating to work things out. She may be mad, but she'll get over it. If you really don't want to belong, I see no reason why you should. Do you want me to speak to her?"

"Will you stop appointing yourself as my spokesman," she said sharply. "I can take care of myself." She saw the surprise in Daniel's face at her outburst and quickly amended, "I'm sorry. I'm just so mad that I let her out-maneuver me. I'll go to the meeting. I can always ease myself out. That way we both win. She has the satisfaction of getting me there, and I know in advance that I don't have to stay."

Slowly Daniel said, "I don't think that's the way to go

about it, but if you want to try it, I have no objections. I still think an honest confrontation would be better for both of you."

"I hate open confrontations. I hate the anger and the words that have to be said." Stubbornly she repeated, "I want to do this my way."

She noticed a slight coolness between them as they prepared for bed. She felt guilty at appearing weak before Daniel, but she would not retract her statement. Daniel's good-night kiss was perfunctory, and as she turned over to her side of the bed, a lonely tear slid down her cheek.

But the next morning things were back to normal. Carole got Daniel off to work and planned her day, beginning with calling Janet Rogers for dinner Friday night. Delightedly Janet accepted the invitation and the time was set.

After the phone call Carole began her baking for Saturday's bake sale, reasoning that she could freeze the cakes until Saturday morning. The kitchen smelled heavenly and she was filled with satisfaction as she carefully placed the cooled items in the freezer. Daniel had his monthly luncheon with the other pastors in the town, so she snacked as she worked. The laundry, clean-smelling and crisp, was put away with a smile, and she prepared a light supper for Daniel with a joyful heart. She heard his key in the door at five-thirty sharp, and she was waiting for him, scrubbed and clad in his favorite slack set.

"You look like an ad for domestic bliss," he declared as he swept her into his strong arms and kissed her soundly.

"I am, and I await your pleasure, sire. I have prepared food for you, and an evening's entertainment, if you like." Her smile held the promise of an evening's delight, and he followed her into the den where she had laid out their supper in front of a glowing fire. The low table was surrounded by big pillows and the lights were low, making a very romantic setting for a Thursday night supper. He gave her a searching look and sank down on one of the pillows, pulling her down with him.

"This is the way to live," he said against her mouth.

"This is the way I want it always to be for us," she said, returning his kiss.

.

Hours later as Carole was falling asleep she made herself a promise: *I love him so much that I'll join that altar guild, and I'll enjoy it. It will make things easier for everybody.*

Friday morning she cleaned the house and prepared a rather elaborate meal for the Rogers. Cooking occupied most of the afternoon, but she was pleased with the results.

Janet and Bill Rogers were about the same age as Daniel and very involved in the life of the church. At dinner, everything went smoothly and Carole felt a warm surge of pleasure at the compliments on her skills as cook and hostess. As she served coffee and dessert in front of the fireplace, she observed that the atmosphere was vastly different from that she and Daniel had shared in this room the night before, and she smiled in remembrance.

Though the conversation was pleasant, Carole felt herself stiffen slightly as Janet began talking about the need for new choir members. Carole deftly changed the subject before the woman could pursue the matter.

"Carole," Janet was saying. "You have done a marvelous job of stepping into the role of pastor's wife. You are a great asset to our church as well as a fine wife for Daniel. The people generally seem to be delighted with your marriage," she said warmly.

Dropping her eyes demurely, Carole murmured an embarrassed thank-you, but she did pick up on the word *generally*. Were there some members who were not happy? "It isn't easy to please everyone," she confessed.

Janet laughed outright. "You'll never do that entirely, I'm afraid. You've had some competition. But I do think they've made peace with the fact that Daniel has chosen you."

Carole looked at Daniel in confusion. "What do you mean?" she asked. "What kind of competition?"

"Daniel," said Mrs. Rogers, "didn't you tell her?"

It was Daniel's turn to look abashed. "I didn't see any need."

Carole was completely perplexed at his answer. "You all seem to know something that I don't. Please fill me in so I can be amused, too."

"It isn't amusing at all," Daniel began. "Janet inadvertently opened a letter intended for me. She didn't realize it was such a personal letter until it was too late." He took a deep breath. "It was a love letter from one of the women in the congregation. I had no idea that she was infatuated with me. I took Janet into my confidence and she helped me decide what to do."

Bill Rogers added, "The woman is still in the congregation. And her feelings toward Pastor haven't changed. So you see, you can't possibly make *everyone* happy. At least one is jealous of your being Daniel's wife. This woman is also in a position to make trouble for you if she chooses."

"Will you tell me who she is?" Carole looked at Daniel, not sure she wanted to hear his answer.

He considered for a long moment and then said, "I'm afraid you would only feel awkward with her."

"But now I'll suspect every woman but Janet of having designs on my husband," she protested.

Still Daniel was reluctant to tell her. "It's Mrs. Wilson," he admitted finally.

*Pretty, young, sexy Mrs. Wilson*, thought Carole. She had to ask, "But you never encouraged her?"

152

"Of course not." He seemed hurt that she would ask. "She's a married woman, and I certainly never dreamed that anything like this was going on in her head."

"Does her husband know?" she asked miserably.

"I can't answer that. Their marriage is definitely on the rocks, but I don't know if she has confided in him." He tried to assure her lightly, "Don't worry, Carole. It's an occupational hazard, you know."

"I do know. It just never happened to me before."

Janet signaled her husband silently. "I think we'd better be on our way. You two may have some things you'd like to talk out privately. Thank-you for such a wonderful evening. I'm sorry if my careless remark has caused you distress."

"I think you did me a favor," Carole responded. "It's always better to know one's competition." Her attempt to sound flippant didn't quite succeed.

Janet took Carole's hand and, looking at Daniel, said, "Believe me when I say you don't seem to have any competition where *he* is concerned. I've never known him to be so happy."

"I agree completely," said Bill. "And that was a superlative meal."

Carole and Daniel saw them to the door and then turned to look at each other. Carole spoke first.

"I am a little angry that you didn't tell me about Mrs. Wilson, but I think I understand. I'd rather not spend any more time talking about it, though, if you don't mind."

"I don't mind. As a matter of fact, I'm relieved. There's nothing more to say about the whole thing, anyway."

That night in bed, Daniel held her tenderly and she went to sleep knowing that she, above all women, was the one he had chosen.

In the morning she took her baked goods over to the church for the sale. There was a good turnout and business was brisk. She found herself looking with new interest at several of the more attractive women . . . and wondering. *You silly child,* she scolded herself. *These women are all happily married. None of them has designs on your husband.* She shook off her unreasonable suspicions, determined to enjoy their company. Gradually she relaxed and caught the spirit of the day.

When it was getting close to time for the sale to end, she spotted Mrs. Wilson browsing through the goodies. The knowledge that this woman was secretly in love with Daniel was still too new. Carole managed to stay busy in the kitchen until Mrs. Wilson had paid for her selections and left. *Someday when I'm grown up, I won't have to hide like this,* thought Carole ruefully. *I just hope I grow up before I'm ninety-eight, so I get a chance to enjoy life.*

"Here you are. I never thought to look in the kitchen." It was Mrs. Charles with her foot in her mouth as usual.

"I brought back your plate. The cake was delicious." Carole handed her the china platter.

"Thank-you. I'm sure when you get back in practice, you'll be a good cook, too." Carole covered a smile. "Did Pastor enjoy it? I just love cooking for a man."

"Yes, he said to tell you that he always enjoys your cakes—and your visits," she added. "He said you always make him smile." Her face was totally without guile.

Mrs. Charles lit up with pleasure. "Did he really? Well, you tell him I'll bring him another cake soon."

"Oh, please do. I'll be ready for you this time." Mrs. Charles looked blank. "I mean the house won't be so messy. I've finished all my fall cleaning."

Mrs. Charles beamed. "I was just telling Joanie Forga the other day that you were fortunate not to have any little ones. They can take up so much of your time."

Mrs. Charles didn't seem to notice that Carole had turned

pale at her thoughtless remark. She started to rattle on, but Carole mumbled, "Excuse me. I see my husband coming," and hurried away swiftly to meet him.

"Are you all right, Carole?" he asked as he saw her stricken face.

"Of course, but I am tired. Could we just go outside for a little fresh air?" He led her outside to a shady place under a magnolia tree.

"Want to tell me what our resident hoof-and-mouth artist said to upset you so?"

"She didn't mean any harm. She was just trying to make conversation. She has no idea how hard it is for me to accept the fact that I can't have children." A tear threatened to spill down her cheek.

"Sometimes I wonder about some of God's people—the ones who seem to do nothing but hurt others. I'm sorry, Carole, that she made you so unhappy." He took her into his arms.

"It's all right, Daniel, really it is. It just took me by surprise. It probably won't be the last time," she added with resignation.

"Probably not. Why don't we just go home? I think you've done all you can do for one day."

## CHAPTER 11

SOMETHING WAS TUGGING AT Carole, drawing her from a deep sleep. She resisted unsuccessfully. When the light hit her in the face, she surrendered her sleep to find Daniel fumbling for the insistently ringing telephone. The clock read 2 A.M.

"Yes," he answered groggily. "That's all right . . . I'm sorry to hear that. Is her husband with her? . . . Good. Yes, I'll be there as soon as I can. Thank-you for calling." He crawled from bed and began to pull on his clothes. "Mrs. Gerhardt is dying," he explained to Carole. "It's only a matter of time."

"I'll go with you," she said, instantly alert and running a comb through her tousled hair.

In a short time they were hurrying to the hospital. Carole felt thoroughly chilled as they drove up to the brightly lit building, for the hospital reminded her of a lonely fortress fighting off death in the night.

The family circle met them with grim expressions of fading hope. It would be Daniel's job to remind them of the

Resurrection and to comfort them in their loss. He shook hands with each family member and went quickly into Mrs. Gerhardt's room. Carole waited outside, helpless to give these grieving people the consolation she longed to provide. She sat beside Mr. Gerhardt, her eyes averted from his somber face. He reached for her hand, and she swallowed hard and took a deep breath, bracing herself to say the words she prayed would be the right ones. But Mr. Gerhardt spoke first.

"This is very hard for you, isn't it, my dear? I know you want to say the right thing, but you needn't worry. It is enough that you are here." He sighed deeply. "My Martha will soon be going to be with Him, so I'm not sad about that. I'm just sad that I'm going to be left behind. Your coming tonight assures me that I am loved, that He has sent me special comfort. Thank-you."

Carole's throat constricted and a tear traced its way down her cheek. She squeezed his hand a little tighter and sat with him until Daniel came out of the room.

"You'd better go in now, George. She's asking for you."

Carole watched Daniel move among the members of the family, radiating strength and hope. Their expressions changed visibly as he prayed with them. And when Mr. Gerhardt joined them a short time later, his demeanor was composed. Though there were tears in his eyes as he told them good-by, his handshake was firm.

"I'll be by in the morning to talk with you about the arrangements, George. She was a fine Christian woman, and I'm happy you had so many years together. I know you'll miss her terribly."

"Thank you, Pastor. Good-night, Carole."

As they left the hospital Carole thought it looked less like a fortress fighting death and more like a warm haven.

They got up at their usual time, for Carole had altar guild, and Daniel had his usual work, plus the funeral sermon to write and the condolence call to make.

"I hope they start this meeting with strong black coffee," she grumbled.

There *was* coffee perking at the church when Carole arrived. It helped to lift her sagging spirits. She was introduced as "our good Pastor's wife" and made to feel welcome. The meeting was devoted to the study of the proper procedure for preparing communion. Carole had belonged to an altar guild before, but never one that had devoted so much time to the exact art of the work. It was interesting, but she was still tired from their late-night hospital visit and found it hard to concentrate. The topic of discussion over coffee centered around Mrs. Gerhardt's death.

"As much as I hate to lose Martha," said one young matron, "I'm glad her suffering is finally over."

"Martha is one person we'll miss around here. She was always such a shining example of a Christian lady," said another.

It was agreed that a memorial fund should be set up immediately by her many friends and relatives. Carole was warmed by the love and consideration shown by the women and felt a deep sense of loss at having been denied the opportunity to know her better.

The church was crowded the next day for the funeral service. Both the ladies' groups had worked together to provide the meal following the committal service, and it was late in the afternoon before Carole finally got home.

She made herself a glass of iced mint tea and took it out on the patio into the crisp fall air. She was reflecting over events of the past hours when she heard the phone ringing. Hurrying inside, she answered a little breathlessly.

"Hello, Mrs. Thornton," came a voice which Carole recognized as belonging to Ellie, the organist. "I called to let you know that my sister will be getting married in two weeks and, since I'll be away, I'm going to need you to play for the Sunday church services." Without waiting for Carole's reply, she continued, "I'm so glad you're going to help me out. I just didn't know what I was going to do until you agreed to help."

"I'm not so sure you'd be glad if you knew how long it has been since I've played for a church service," Carole said weakly.

"You'll do fine. And, Mrs. Thornton, would you consider helping me on a regular basis? Maybe every other month. There just isn't anyone else qualified to do it." Her voice took on a plaintive tone. "I've played for a lot of services when I was sick, and once I even played with a broken finger. I sure need someone I can depend on."

"But—" Carole began.

Ellie hurried on. "Please, It's just gotten to be too much for one person."

"You make it hard to say no. I'll help you at least until we can find someone else." Carole's voice was resigned.

"Thank-you. I just *knew* you wouldn't let me down."

Carole hung up and made a careful note on her calendar, which she noticed was becoming alarmingly full. *I can do it,* she chided herself. *I'm not working at a regular job anymore.*

Wednesday came and went with the midweek prayer service as the final activity of the week. Upon checking the calendar once more, however, Carole was reminded that Thursday was her first meeting with the afternoon ladies' group. As the telephone chairman, she spent all of Thursday morning trying to reach the members to remind them.

The meeting was well attended and the agenda was full. Each lady had brought a sample of handcrafts or needlework for the bazaar to be held later in the month. Carole, of course, had nothing with her, but volunteered to bake something. Surely, with a full week to go, she could work a little baking into her schedule, she thought. Armed with some mouth-watering recipes from some of the best cooks in the church, she left the meeting feeling buoyant and eager to get started on her project.

As she was about to step into her car, she heard Joyce call out, "Carole, I'll see you Saturday morning for the general clean-up. Do you want me to pick you up, or are you coming with Daniel?"

"Clean-up? Oh, no! I'd forgotten all about that! Joyce, tell me the truth. Do I have to come? I have so many things I really need to do," she pleaded.

"Do what you want." Joyce shrugged. "But the pastor's wife *always* helps with fall clean-up."

"I can't believe you said that. Of all people, I thought *you'd* understand." said Carole a little sharply.

"Understand what?"

"That I'm a different pastor's wife, and that I don't have time to come up here and clean a building that's practically spotless already." She cooled down a bit and apologized. "I just can't make it, Joyce, if I'm going to get these things done for the bazaar.

"Okay, Carole. Don't worry about it. I'll cover for you and there will be plenty of volunteers. I know you can't do everything," she relented. "And I know you're a different pastor's wife. I promise never to say that to you again. Friends?"

"Friends. And I'm sorry I got huffy. I think I'm a little overscheduled. I'll call you next week and we'll have some of those little pecan pies."

"You do know my weaknesses. Better make it the first of the week, since Thanksgiving is this next Thursday. How about Monday?" she calculated mentally.

"Can't. That's Daniel's day off and we've already made plans. Tuesday?"

"No, I'm busy that day, and Wednesday is really not good, either. My parents are coming in that night. Are you having company?"

"No, we plan to celebrate quietly this year. Daniel and I may even take some time off and drive down to the coast."

"A second honeymoon already? How romantic," she smiled slyly.

"It seems we'll just have to wait until after the holidays then. Sorry, Joyce."

They parted with regret and promises to get together soon. *Things will settle down after this bazaar,* Carole hoped.

Friday and Saturday were spent in baking for the bazaar, but Carole was pleased with the results of her labors. When she woke up on Sunday morning, she couldn't believe it was time to start the week all over again. Having the promise of all day Monday with Daniel eased the hectic Sunday schedule, and she felt a sense of relief that she didn't have to teach Sunday school again.

After church she noticed that Mrs. Wilson was spending an inordinate amount of time with Daniel, talking in serious tones. Carole waited until they were finished with their conversation before approaching him.

"What was that all about?" she asked with a teasing gleam in her eye.

"Polly wants to talk to me. She's quite upset about her separation from her husband."

"I'm sorry to hear that," Carole said, not unkindly.

"The bad news is that tomorrow is the only day she can

161

come in to the office. Now Carole," he said, catching her expression of dismay, "before you say anything, let me tell you that I tried to set up the meeting at a different time, but it just wasn't possible."

"It's really all right, Daniel," Carole struggled to sound convincing. "I have a lot of things I need to do, anyway. It will give me another day to work on some other items for the bazaar. Let's go home and eat our roast before we have another burnt offering."

But all day Monday Carole felt waves of frustration, knowing that Daniel was closeted away with Polly Wilson while she stuck her finger with a needle and tried to bake another cake at the same time. "I'm not jealous," she muttered to herself. "I'm just irritated that she took him away from me on the only day we really have to call our own. She's in trouble and I know he has to try to help her, buh she could have planned her crisis a little more conveniently," she thought unreasonably.

She had just stuck herself for the third time when the phone rang. As she walked over to answer it, she said, "I think I'm beginning to hate you, you little black monster." Into the receiver she spoke pleasantly, "Hello."

"Hello. Is my dad there?" There was a moment of silence while Carole tried to place the voice.

"Oh, Leigh! No, he's at the church. Can I help you with something?"

Now there was silence on the other end of the line. "No, I don't think so. I need to talk to my dad. I'll just call him there." She had hung up before Carole could tell her that her father was busy and shouldn't be disturbed.

"I would have been glad to talk with you for a few minutes if you had given me the chance," she said into the dead receiver. Sighing, she replaced the phone in its cradle.

When Daniel came home for a late lunch, Carole was

dying of curiosity about Polly Wilson and about Leigh's call.

"Is everything all right?" she asked anxiously.

"Yes and no," was his reply. "Leigh asked if she could come home for Thanksgiving. Apparently she's having difficulties at school, but didn't seem to want to talk about it over the phone, so I'll just have to wait until she gets here. It is all right?" he asked, almost as an afterthought.

"Of course," Carole's response was genuinely enthusiastic, until a tiny spasm of anxiety rippled in the pit of her stomach. "It will give us a chance to get to know each other. If she's anything like you, I can't help loving her." *But will she even like me,* fretted Carole. *She's stayed away so long.*

Daniel took her in his arms. "Since I cheated you out of our day together, how about dinner out tonight? I know this charming little place with a romantic atmosphere. It could be the start of a wonderful evening." His handsome face smiled down at her, and she felt all his warmth and love enveloping her.

"Sounds great. I guess I could use a little comforting myself."

He looked steadily at her. "Carole, you look tired. Maybe you should back off a little—just a little," he added, seeing the warning look in her face. "You weren't called as the assistant pastor, you know."

"Yes, dear, I hear you. Don't worry about me. I'm just tired. But not too tired to go out to dinner with a handsome fellow."

She proved herself to be a poor prophet, for she fell asleep in the car on the way home.

"I just need a good night's sleep," she protested as Daniel tucked her into bed.

"Yes, love, I know. Sleep well."

163

Carole awoke in the morning, feeling rested and ready for the day. Humming as she prepared a festive breakfast, she made some mental notes.

"What's all this? Is it Thanksgiving morning already?" Daniel's smile was wide and cheerful as he sat down to the bountiful table.

"No," she said sheepishly. "I'm just trying to make up for falling asleep last night."

"Could we arrange for that to happen more often?" he teased. "I like the way you make up."

"When is Leigh coming and how long will she be staying?" Carole changed the subject adroitly.

Daniel put down his steaming cup of coffee. "She's driving in tomorrow morning, but I'm not sure how long she plans to stay. I guess it depends on the seriousness of her problem." He looked worried.

"Oh, when she arrives is no problem for me. I'm just trying to make plans for food and I want the guest room to be especially nice for her." She put their plates on the table and sat down across from him.

"Do you mind her coming like this, Carole?"

"To be honest, I'm more nervous than anything."

"I have the feeling *she's* nervous, too, and embarrassed at meeting you for the first time under these circumstances." Daniel took a bite of the fluffy pancake on his plate.

"You know I'll do my best to make her feel at home, Daniel. I do want her to feel that this is her home to come back to whenever she wants."

"You're a warm and caring woman, Carole." His gaze encompassed her with love.

"I live with a good example," she responded. "Now finish your breakfast and let me get on with my work."

By ten o'clock Carole had the house clean and the guest

But as soon as Mrs. Charles was safely down the walk, Carole stomped down the hallway to the kitchen and picked up the prune cake. Ceremoniously she dumped it into the sink and smiled as she poured soap on it and then flushed the entire gooey mess down the food disposal unit with hot water. She washed and dried the plate and put it away carefully in the cabinet where Daniel wouldn't see it. Still, she was angry. Taking the untouched tea glasses, she poured their contents out into the sink, too. She looked at the pretty glasses of which she had been so proud, and knew she would never be able to use them again without remembering this unhappy day, then sat down at the table and began to cry. Her chest hurt as if Mrs. Charles had stabbed her with real knives instead of only sharp words. *I'm trying. I'm doing the best I can. Why is she so hateful? Why does she take such delight in cutting me down?* The tears turned into sobs, and she laid her head on the table, soaking the cloth with her misery.

Eventually she sat up, spent, and reached for a napkin to dry her eyes. It was then that she smelled smoke. For a moment she couldn't think why there would be smoke in the house. "My cake!" she cried, racing for the belching oven. "Oh, no, not my cake, too!" Her tears started anew as she took out the charred remains of her lovely cake. There was nothing to do but add it to the list of casualties down the food disposal unit.

Resolutely she began mixing the ingredients for another cake. By the time it was ready for the oven, she had dried her tears, but the joy had fled from the day. She freshened her make-up and tried to force the unhappy experience away so Daniel would find her cheerful when he came home for supper.

She met him at the door with a smile. "Hi, love, how was your day?"

"Pretty good. How was yours?"

"Very busy. I forgot to take my cake out, and I burned it. So I had to start over from scratch. All in all, not a very productive day, I'm afraid." She sounded so forlorn that Daniel took her in his arms.

"There's no point in upsetting yourself about a silly cake. Did something else happen today?" he asked suspiciously.

"No, of course not. I just hate to burn anything. Your supper is ready and you'd better eat if you want to get to the Board of Education meeting on time. Pastors are not supposed to be late."

He looked at her, puzzled, but he didn't probe further into her dark mood.

"The house looks lovely, Carole. I can see you spent a lot of time getting ready for Leigh's visit. Thanks for caring so much."

"I just want everything to be so right for her."


In the fireplace the fire crackled merrily. A low table in front of it was set for light refreshments. Everything was in order, but Carole prowled the room, fussing over little things. She glanced at Daniel who was seated in his favorite chair, reading the evening paper with his feet propped up to the fire. *Well,* she mused, *at least it's half a scene of domestic tranquillity.* Carole felt a surge of relief when at last the doorbell sounded, putting an end to the waiting. They walked together to the front door to welcome Daniel's daughter.

"Hello, Dad."

Leigh was almost as tall as her father, but her long hair was a soft golden blond and her eyes a lighter hazel brown. She was fashionably dressed and quite beautiful. Carole liked her instantly.

"Leigh, come in! We thought you'd never get here. How

was your trip? Here, let me take your coat." Daniel was obviously delighted to see her. Carole stepped forward and Daniel slipped his arm around her. "Leigh, this is Carole."

Leigh offered her hand with a perfunctory smile. "Hello." Her voice was cool.

Leigh's formality failed to ease Carole's anxiety. *I wish I'd worn my new silk blouse,* she thought.

"I'm so glad to meet you—finally—" Carole began, then paused miserably, realizing she had not intended for her greeting to sound like a scolding. "Come on in here by the fire and warm yourself. There is tea, or coffee if you prefer."

Carole led the way and Leigh followed her to the fireplace, extending her hands to its warmth. "Your home is very nice," she said politely. "I see Dad brought all his books with him." Her eyes swept the room as if searching for more evidence of his presence. Carole watched as Leigh's gaze fell on her own graduation picture standing on a small table.

"I want you to feel at home here, Leigh," she said. "I know it must seem strange to you now, but please feel free to consider this your second home."

Carole handed her a cup of coffee and made a mental note as the girl added cream and sugar. Pouring two more cups, she handed one to Daniel. The cups rattled a bit in their saucers, an audible clue to her tension.

Daniel gave her an encouraging grin and settled back in his chair. "How's school, Leigh?" he asked casually, turning to his daughter.

Her carefully masked expression didn't change. "Fine. I've just been working too hard. That's why I decided to take a short holiday."

*She definitely doesn't want to talk in front of me,* thought Carole, and after what she hoped was a polite interval, she stifled a yawn and excused herself. "Would you mind if I turn in early, dear?" she asked Daniel. "It's been a long day and I want to be rested for tomorrow." To Leigh she said, "Your father and I are so pleased you came. Everything is ready for you, but if you need anything else, just ask. See you both in the morning."

It was hours later when Daniel finally slid into bed beside her.

"That was a wonderful thing you did." He pulled her over against him. "Leigh felt reluctant to expose her 'failures,' as she called them, to you just yet."

"Did you get anything worked out?"

"Yes, I would say we had a fruitful visit, but right now I'm too bushed to go into details."

"I didn't expect a blow-by-blow account anyway," she said a little defensively. "Good night." *What did they talk about all that time? Obviously Leigh's problems. Me, too? Oh, go to sleep, child, just go to sleep,* she fussed at herself.

Thanksgiving morning blew in gray and windy. There was even a hint of snow in the air, a rarity for East Texas. It reminded Carole of the "blue northers" of the Panhandle area where she grew up. Everyone bundled up tight for the short drive to the special morning service. Daniel's sermon was moving, and Carole was keenly aware of the many blessings she had to count this day. Her love for Daniel was never greater, and she was sure she was loved in equal measure. She had a harder time counting the blessings of the congregation they served.

Glancing around the congregation, she spotted Tillie. *I can never be too careful what I say around her,* she cautioned herself. And there was Mr. Wilcott's dour face. Maybe simply avoiding him would be the better part of valor. Somehow he always seemed to make her feel like a guilty child. There were the women who had insisted she join their ladies' groups—because they liked her, or because it was her duty? The organist appeared in her peripheral vision. Soon it would be her turn up there. The idea frightened her. *I'm not sure I can play for the services again,* she thought. *And over there sits a woman who will call me far too often to take her Sunday school classes. Where is Polly Wilson? Is she still in love with my husband?* Covertly, she looked to her left. *And who are the women who are gossiping about it?* But most depressing of all, there right in front of her sat Mrs. Charles—the woman who had made her so angry, and who had planted an ugly seed in Carole's mind. Who were all the women who had criticized her for not being there for cleaning day? Had none defended her? Did they smile at her, and then talk about her behind her back? Which ones? Carole began to feel faint. She took careful, deep breaths. *Stop! Stop this nonsense. These people are your family.* She looked around for the people she really liked and trusted. There were many. But the negative things kept popping into her mind. *Even Daniel's daughter has not accepted me. Lord,* she prayed, *please help me to rise above this pettiness. Fill me with Your love, so I can love even the unlovable. Give me the strength to be a good pastor's wife for Daniel's sake—and for Yours.* She felt a little better after her prayer.

But as the service drew to a close, Carole felt a real reluctance to mingle with the people. Instead of moving from group to group as she usually did, she hurried to Daniel's study, telling herself she needed to hurry home to put the finishing touches on their Thanksgiving dinner. Even Daniel's study did not provide her with the refuge she sought, for people were moving in and out, and it seemed to take forever before they were finally on their way home.

Though the dinner she had so carefully prepared looked

festive, the talk around the table was not. Leigh was polite, but distant. If they had spoken about Daniel's marriage last night, it hadn't changed anything. Carole felt as dreary as the day looked. The only thing that kept the occasion from being a total disaster was Daniel's determination to keep the mood light with hilarious stories of parishioners from past congregations.

The phone rang and Daniel took the call. There was an apology in his eyes as he returned from the brief conversation. "Carole, I know this is a special day, but I must go out for a little while. That was Polly's husband. She has locked herself in the bedroom with a gun. I think you know I have to go."

"Can't the police handle it? This *is* Thanksgiving," she said through stiff lips.

"You should know better than that!" Anger and frustration glinted from his eyes. "You'd also better pray that I say the right things to her," he called sharply over his shoulder as he went out the door. "I'll be home when all this is resolved with Polly, but don't look for me anytime soon." He slammed the door loudly on his way out.

The only thing Carole could think was: *That's the first time he's ever left the house without kissing me good-by*. Something splintered inside her, way down deep, like a crack in a board.

Carole began cleaning off the table, and a silent Leigh joined her. She tried to make small talk, to apologize for the angry exchange the girl had overheard, but was met with monosyllabic answers. She gave up and went into the kitchen to load the dishwasher. Leigh followed her, carrying more dishes, her face set in the mask she apparently wore for strangers.

*If I could only get past that cool reserve*, thought Carole.

172

*If she would just give me a chance, I know we could be friends*. Deciding to give it one more try, she turned to Leigh and said pleasantly, "Your mother must have been a wonderful woman."

Leigh looked directly at her and replied, "Yes, she was—and no one could ever take her place."

Embarrassed at the rebuff, Carole said, "I'm sure of that, Leigh. I don't want to take her place, but I would hope that you would at least let me be a part of your life. I've never had a daughter, and I have so much I want to share. I'd like to share it with you." With this baring of her heart, tears welled up in her eyes.

Incredulous eyes stared back at her. "Do you honestly think I could ever be your substitute daughter—the daughter I suspect a busy woman like you chose not to have?" Ice sheathed her last words. "Never, never, ever!" and she turned on her heels and fled in anger. A door slammed hard down the hallway.

Carole stood frozen with the harsh rejection. *I didn't choose!* she thought wildly. *I didn't choose!* Her last bulwark gave way inside and she felt the world come crashing down around her. She ran, tear-blinded, to her bedroom. Her thoughts were incoherent, but her instincts told her to run—away from all pain and mistrust. She grabbed a suitcase from the closet, throwing clothes in it, then ravaged her dressing table and bathroom, piling the items helter-skelter into a smaller case. Tearing her coat from a hanger, she raced down the hallway, grabbed her purse from the small marble table, and fled to her car. Sharp sobs tore at her chest and she had difficulty in seeing to insert the ignition key. "No more pain," she mumbled. "I can't take any more pain." She wiped the tears from her eyes with bloodless hands and started driving, not sure of her destination. *I'm so cold, and I hurt so badly. Must get warm.* And she headed to the place where she had found warmth with Daniel. Galveston. Happy times. Love.

For five hours she drove as if all the demons in hell were in pursuit. When she finally pulled up in front of the realty office in Jamaica Beach, it was closed. Total despair was edging in on her when she spotted an emergency number posted on the door. In minutes she was inside a public phone booth, pleading for help. The woman named Janice was friendly despite the inopportune hour, and agreed to come to the office.

Shortly Carole was carrying her suitcases up the stairs of a tiny beach house. Unlocking the door, she located the bedroom and dropped her things on the bed. Now that she was in a place she deemed safe, she began to feel the overwhelming sense of panic slip away from her and she was startled to feel that the room was bitterly cold. Shivering, she searched for matches to light the furnace. Then she slipped off her shoes and crawled fully clothed into bed, pulling several blankets over her for added warmth. With the warmth came blessed sleep.

## CHAPTER 12

CAROLE AWOKE, DISORIENTED. Struggling to a sitting position, she was surprised to find herself still dressed. She slipped off her coat and hung it in the small closet, smoothed down the wrinkled dress, and padded barefoot to the kitchen.

*There must be some coffee here somewhere,* she thought. She found an individually wrapped packet in a drawer and boiled some water. *I can see I'm going to have to get some supplies if I stay here. What did I tell that woman last night? How long did I say I was staying?* Everything was a blur. She rummaged through her handbag and found a receipt for a week's rental. A week—at least.

Shame flooded her as she pondered Daniel's state of mind right now. *I can't go back yet. I can't bear to face him.* She considered calling him, but the idea of hearing his voice immobilized her. *He'll talk me into going back. And I can't. I just can't! Or maybe he won't care if I come back or not.* The sudden thought was chilling.

Carole's conscience nagged at her until she got in the car

and drove to the public pay phone. Placing a collect call to Joyce, she rested her head in one hand until the call went through.

"Carole! What in the world is going on? Where are you?"

"Just listen, Joyce. I want you to let Daniel know I'm fine. Tell him I'm on my way to Lubbock to stay with a friend and I'll call him in a few days."

"Lubbock! Carole, what happened?"

"Please. Just tell him what I said." Carole's voice broke. "Tell him I need a little time to think things out. Please, Joyce. Good-by." She hung up quickly before her friend could question her further. Then she stood there in the cold phone booth, crying silently.

When she opened the door of the booth, she could hear the surf pounding the beach and the piercing, shrill cries of the gulls. The cold salty air brought color to her cheeks, and deep breaths of it fueled her resolve to keep going. *I'll get a few groceries and eat a good breakfast,* she thought. *Then I'll decide what to do next.* Formulating a plan of action gave her some feeling of order and taking control of her life again.

Thus fortified, Carole hurried to Red's, a small, all-purpose market she had discovered on her honeymoon. But after breakfast she was exhausted and she crawled back into bed and slept hard.

It was late evening when she finally woke again. The house felt chilly and she built a fire in the little fireplace and sat in front of it, hugging her knees. *I need to think this out,* she determined. *I need to think about Daniel.* Daniel. Daniel . . . Even his name brought quick tears to her eyes.

She nibbled at some cheese and crackers and sipped strong coffee. Still she fell asleep in front of the fire and roused only when the fire burned itself out. *Why can't I stay*

176

*awake?* she fretted. *I've slept most of the day away.* With a start she recalled that yesterday had been Thanksgiving Day. It seemed like a million light years ago.

Carole rebuilt the fire and drowsed in front of it until dawn. Then she bundled up tightly and walked out on the beach to watch the sunrise. The sky was tinted delicate shades of peach and orange and blue. Then, as the sun rose higher in the sky, the horizon turned a glorious gold. The brisk wind blowing off the water kept the sun from warming the beach, and soon the biting cold drove her back inside. But the sea air had invigorated her, and now she felt the need to grapple with her flight.

Her mind carefully chose only one piece of the puzzle. Daniel. How angry he had been with her, and how unlike him. Why didn't he understand that she needed him as much as Polly? He had left her to care for someone else. *That's part of the reason I love him. He cares so much for everyone. But I do love him. Of that one thing I'm sure.*

Still the troublesome thoughts roiled in her mind. *I want to be married to Daniel, but I can't go back to being a pastor's wife. The congregation is not any better or any worse than others I've known, and I love being with most of the people. But I can't handle the criticism and unkindness of the few who seem to make their life's work causing problems for others.* She shook her head at the utter futility of her dilemma.

She picked up another piece of the puzzle. *Leigh. I wanted so much for her to accept me.* She laughed a mirthless laugh. *Perhaps I did want to replace her mother. I thought I'd die when the doctor first said I could never have a baby. If only Samuel had consented to adopt a child, how different things might have been.*

Then, unbidden, a scene floated back to her. She and Daniel, newly married, were standing among a group of women at the church. Everyone was full of good wishes and congratulations when one sweet grandmotherly woman commented, "Now, the only thing you need to make your happiness complete is a family, but then maybe you're one of those liberated women." How those words had stung. But Carole had smiled and gone on pleasantly with the conversation, never revealing the depth of her pain. *Leigh could have been that long-desired daughter*, thought Carole, *but she has made it clear she doesn't want me in her family*. A deep sense of sadness engulfed her. *The two things I want most are out of my reach. Daniel and Leigh.* In her despair she cried herself to sleep. Sleep was her refuge, for it was dreamless and painless.

On Sunday morning she woke with a sense of urgency. But she had nowhere to go and nothing to do. For the first time in a very long time, she was totally free of responsibility—and she felt guilty. She should be in the kitchen, frying bacon for Daniel's breakfast and preparing their noon meal. She should be getting dressed for Sunday school and church. Was this her Sunday to play the organ for the service? Shame crept over her when she recalled that it was. What would Daniel tell the people when she didn't appear? She wondered if Leigh were still there.

Mentally she went through the morning routine with Daniel. Nine o'clock. He would be leaving for the church. Ten-thirty. He would be walking out of his study to the altar to begin the church service. What text would he use for his sermon? Marital fidelity? They would all be there. Her friends and her accusers. How many meetings would she miss in the next few days, or would it be longer? The bazaar! It was yesterday! All her baked goods were still in the freezer, unless of course, someone thought to ask for them. Then she realized ruefully that Dr. Heckmann had been there on Friday for the Fall Workshop. She had planned to bake blueberry muffins for him. Had Daniel confided in him about their problems? Pastors have so few people they can risk with their troubles, she knew. But it was possible that Daniel wasn't even looking for her. Maybe he had decided that her leaving was best for both of them. Her misery was boundless.

The wind had dropped and she decided to brave the beach once more. She was surprised to find that it was almost warm now. Her eyes scanned the edge of the water, coming to rest on a shark's tooth. It was pointed at the end, and she could imagine the fierce mouth from which it had come. It reminded her of the people who had hurt her, their mouths tearing and devouring the soft flesh of her heart. She dropped the tooth in her coat pocket as a visual reminder of what she had left behind. The large diamond ring on her left hand served to remind her of the good part.

But the diamond distracted her, for it kept sparkling in the bright sunlight, a beacon calling her home to Daniel. She remembered the joyous day she had received it. And her wedding day. What happy times those had been. *What has happened to the time? Was it I who changed?* Her question revolved over and over in her mind, begging for but never receiving an answer. *Am I happier now? No, not happier, but more peaceful. Liar!* accused her heart. It was true that she was not under stress to meet all her obligations, but the peace was not there, for neither was Daniel.

By nightfall she had decided to contact Daniel. There was no telephone in the house, but she could never say on the phone all that she wanted to tell him. She sat down at the desk in the living room and drew pen and paper from the drawer. There were several abortive attempts before she finished the letter to her satisfaction. Then, not waiting for morning, she drove to the little post office and mailed it.

Later, as she lay down to sleep, Carole was content that she had done the right thing. If Daniel loved her and still wanted her, he would come to her.

Four long days passed—days in which she walked the lonely beach, watching angry waves assault the shoreline. There was a storm brewing in the gulf, and it had an ominous feeling about it. Carole knew it was not impossible for a hurricane to blow up this time of the year, and she debated the wisdom of staying. She had seen no signs of the islanders leaving, although she did notice more traffic headed toward the little grocery stores on Jamaica Beach. *I'll have to make a decision soon,* she thought. *The house is rented for only one more day. If I haven't heard from him by then, I'll have to decide what to do.*

She struggled with a disembodied feeling as she looked down the road of her life, recognizing no signposts. She had been alone before, but she'd had no choice in the matter then—Samuel was dead. Daniel was alive, but the separation seemed more final than death. Maybe he didn't want her any more. To be rejected by the man she loved would be worse—so much worse. Even her prayers had seemingly rebounded from heaven. She had never felt so desolate.

Carole turned to walk back to the house, dodging the edge of the greedy waves. As she drew nearer, she saw a man standing on the beach in front of the house. Daniel? Her hopes rose. It couldn't be Daniel, for this man slumped instead of standing straight and tall. This man appeared haggard, unshaven. Even at a distance she could see that his clothes were rumpled. Probably a derelict. She was seized by a moment of panic.

Catching sight of her, the man began to take long strides toward her, quickly closing the distance between them.

"Carole! Carole!" he shouted.

"Daniel? Is that you, Daniel?" She was running now to

those open arms. The strong arms reached for her, crushing her against a hard chest, and the mouth kissed her hungrily and then murmured her name over and over. Carole was laughing and crying.

"Thank God I've found you!" Daniel exulted, and in the next minute he was furious. "Don't you ever do that to me again! Don't you ever leave me even to buy groceries without telling me where you're going. Oh, Carole, I don't know whether to hug you or beat you. I've been like a crazy man! Carole, my darling Carole!" His tears mingled with hers, and they held each other as a low rumbling of thunder swiftly followed a vivid slash of lightning, illuminating the turbulent sea.

"Come inside," Carole said. "Come inside out of the storm—and let me love you. I want to feel you hold me so close to your heart that I am almost a part of it." They started up the stairs. "But first let me explain—" Carole began.

"Hush. Don't say anything except that you love me and will never leave me again." he interrupted. "There will be time later for explanations."

The storm came crashing down on the little house, but its fury was well matched by the passion of their love. The wind howled and the rain began to pound the roof, while inside Carole's tears of joy flowed freely. They clung together, making promise after promise and thanking God for the beauty of their reunion. And though the storm threatened to blow the little house into the Gulf, Carole wasn't afraid.

Later, curled in front of the fire, Daniel told Carole that he had arranged to take off the next three days. "I think we're going to need some time together to work out our problems," he explained.

"Daniel, that's wonderful!" Carole cried. "Now, are you ready to hear me out?"

"Yes—it's time we talked."

"The first thing I want you to know is that I truly do love you," she began.

"I think you made that abundantly clear," Daniel teased. "Don't ever change."

Her cheeks colored slightly, but she refused to drop her steady gaze. "That's the only thing about our life together that I wouldn't want to change," she stated flatly, "but the rest isn't going to be so easily solved." She paused and hid her face in his chest.

"What do you want changed, Carole? I can't promise you that I will always be able to stay home with you if someone really needs me. Polly. . . ."

"Oh, it isn't Polly—well, not *only* Polly." She searched for a way to express her feelings. "You left that day without kissing me good-by," she finished feebly.

"That isn't the whole story. It was Leigh, wasn't it?"

"Yes, I guess Leigh was the final straw." Carole sat up in agitation. "I tried so hard to reach her, Daniel. I told her I didn't want to replace her mother, that I just wanted to be part of her life." Great drops splashed down her cheeks. "She told me she would never, ever let me into her life." Carole fell against his broad chest, sobbing openly.

"Leigh told me everything after I got back from Polly's," he said, his lips against her hair. "She didn't spare herself, Carole. She admitted to me that she had lashed out at you in anger, to hurt you. She knew she couldn't do anything about our marriage, but she was determined not to do anything to lessen her mother's importance in her life.

"Carole, she came back home because the young man she loves broke her heart. She had no one left but me." He shifted until he could look directly into Carole's tear-stained face. "When she saw how much we loved each other, she was jealous. Leigh came home, hoping to find things the way they used to be. Instead, she found me, not alone and unhappy like she, but filled with new life. She broke down and cried and begged me to forgive her. She's waiting for the chance to ask you the same thing." There was a catch in his voice. He paused before going on.

"Leigh didn't have to call me when your letter came. But she saw her father nearly go out of his mind with worry, so she helped me find you. She could have just thrown the letter away."

Carole shuddered at the thought of her fate in the hands of his angry daughter. "I want to see her, to try again to make her understand."

"Now she is the one who wants to make you understand. She wants another chance. You two can work it out when we get home."

"But you don't understand, Daniel. I *can't* go home," Carole broke into fresh sobs.

"What?"

"It isn't just Leigh—it's everyone else, too. I just can't cope with the people." Panic filled her eyes. "I didn't tell you about Mrs. Charles, or the gossip, or how they hate me for not going to cleaning day, or . . ."

"Whoa. One thing at a time." His brow was wrinkled in consternation. "What about Mrs. Charles?"

His face darkened with anger as Carole recounted the woman's pious words, warning her about her role as a pastor's wife and the gossip about Daniel and Polly. "This time she has gone too far. When I get home, the board of elders and I will deal with her. Why didn't you tell me?" he demanded, his jaw tensed with anger.

"There didn't seem to be any point. I knew there was

"nothing really going on between you and Polly."

"But you let her make you feel like a failure."

"Yes, but what she said was true—at least the part about being a good example. I know I need to be."

His eyes were blazing. "Carole, we don't live under the Law anymore. We live by the gospel, and love is the heart of the gospel. Every word that came out of that woman's mouth was legalism. Can't you see that? I'd like to . . ." He struggled to suppress his rage.

"Daniel!"

"This is called righteous anger, Carole. Even the Lord threw out the moneychangers, and I intend to do a little housecleaning, too!"

"But you can't throw out all the gossips in the church, Daniel. First of all, you don't even know who they are," she argued. "The damage is done. There's no way to protest your innocence with Polly—no way to make the people stop taking potshots at the two of us. We make too good a target."

"Then I'll go back and resign my pastorate. We'll move."

"Daniel, that's very noble of you, but there is one thing we both know. Every congregation has a Tillie, a Miller, a Mrs. Charles, a Polly, and two ladies' groups." She sighed and looked at him helplessly. "I simply can't go through all this again. I was right all along. I guess I just wasn't cut out to be a pastor's wife."

"That doesn't give us much room to navigate, since I love you and intend to stay married to you." He took her in his arms. "Maybe it's time for me to get out of the ministry. Right now I'm feeling very disgusted with the whole thing."

"What would you do?" she asked miserably.

"Sell shoes, be a consultant, learn a trade."

She looked deep into his eyes. "You belong to the Lord, Daniel. You can't just throw all that away because I can't cope with the pressures. You'd be miserable not being among your people, taking care of them, scolding them, loving them."

"I'm not so sure. I've been in the ministry long enough to know that nothing I say or do seems to touch some people. Maybe the Lord is trying to tell me something."

"Daniel, are you really that unhappy, or are you trying to talk yourself out of the ministry for my sake? I've seen the glow of happiness on your face as you move among the people. I've seen you lift them from despair to hope. I've seen the love that flows between you. No, that's not the answer." She shook her head firmly.

"Carole, I'm only a man, and sometimes the price I have to pay for those moments is too great. I need you by my side. Having those things without you is a price I am not willing to pay. I am not turning my back on God for your love. I'm just going to find a new way to serve Him. You don't have to be a minister to be a servant of the Lord. Millions of people do it every day. Now come closer to me and hold me. I want to fall asleep with you in my arms."

Carole lay awake for a long time, relieved that Daniel would not force her to return to the things that had made her so unhappy. Then fear engulfed her. What would he do? Could he really walk away from his ministry and be happy with her, or would he come to hate her after he realized what he had given up for their love?

*What do we do now, Lord,* she prayed. *Everything is in such a mess.* The thunder rolled again as if in agreement. *Lord, all my life you've led me like a little child—a sometimes stubborn and rebellious child. Now you've brought Daniel into my life, and I don't want my selfish desires to hurt him, or to lure him away from what You want him to do. Please, Lord, lead this little child again. Show me what to do.*

There was another answering roll of thunder, and then only the soft caressing sounds of the rain. She knew the Lord had heard her prayer, and whatever happened would be the right thing for them both.


With the morning sun came a resurgence of hope. Carole felt the answer to her prayer would come soon, but neither Daniel nor Carole made any attempt to discuss their problems. It was their holiday—their time to be together without interruption.

They bundled up and tromped the beach, laughing and playing like children. The ocean was still restless from the storm and continued to spew up wreckage with each new wave.

"Daniel, look at this magnificent shell. I've never seen one like it here before."

"Hey, and here's a very old bottle. The barnacles have completely covered this one side."

"Does it have a message in it?" she teased. "Don't look at me like that! Sometimes they do!"

Daniel surveyed the littered beach. "Just look at all this stuff. Garbage, shells, driftwood, ski ropes, pieces of wooden boats, what a mess to be cleaned up."

"It's also possible that there could be a Spanish coin, or something from a wrecked pirate ship." Her eyes were shining with excitement. "This is the first time I've ever been on the beach after such a big storm. I wish we had a metal detector. There's no telling what was washed ashore, or has been uncovered by the waves. Let's go on down the beach to that next section. I always have good luck finding things in front of yellow beach houses."

"You are kidding, aren't you?"

"Nope. Almost every time I've found a really large shark's tooth, it's been in front of a yellow beach house."

They found a rusted watch and one thong sandal with a broken strap.

"So much for yellow beach houses," commented Carole sadly. "Here's a Portuguese man-of-war. Help me bury it in the sand so no one steps on it. How can anything that beautiful be so lethal? Don't touch it, just use that piece of wood to move it around."

She moved eagerly from one pile of refuse to another, but Daniel seemed to be losing interest.

"I think I'm about ready to go back to the house," he said.

"But, Daniel, there might be something really wonderful out there—just waiting for us to find it—if we don't give up!" she protested. Suddenly she stood very still, almost forgetting to breathe. "That's it," she said softly. "That's the answer." Excitement began to flow from her body in almost visual waves. She ran over to a perplexed Daniel, almost dancing. "Don't you see—my life the past few months has been just like this beach. At first, it was tranquil. Then there was a storm, just the way it was for me. Now there is debris everywhere. Some of it is garbage, some of it is deadly, some of it may be valuable, but we sorted through it and took what we wanted. We *chose*."

The dawning of understanding illuminated Daniel's face.

She continued, "I can choose." Her face was radiant with happiness. "I've been choosing the wrong things. Life as a pastor's wife can be what I make it, or I can let all the garbage bury me." She reached up and wrapped her arms around him, covering his face with kisses. I choose—with God's help, to forgive, to love, to grow—with you, Daniel."

"My darling wife. My love. My Carole." He whispered

the words against her mouth. "I wanted our life to be happy for you. I thought I could *make* it happy for you. Now we both know the power comes from God and lies within each of us."

"I can do it, Daniel. I know I can." She sobered a bit and reflected. "I'm not silly enough to think that everything from now on will always be perfect." Almost speaking to herself, she added, "I must take one day at a time." She looked at him squarely. "I want to go home with you and start over. I want to be your wife—first. That's the single most important thing to me, the way I can serve God best. Being a pastor's wife will have to come farther down the list."

Daniel opened his mouth to speak, then closed it. She waited as he started again. "At the risk of making you angry, I must say that I think I've heard that somewhere before."

She burst out laughing. "I hate know-it-all pastors."

"How do you feel about know-it-all husbands?"

"I think I can learn to live with this one, provided he doesn't say 'I told you so' in tactful ways too often."

"At least I was tactful." He looked past her to the still-agitated ocean, his smile one of deep contentment. "There's really only one thing more I need to make me completely happy."

"What's that?"

"Lunch."

## CHAPTER 13

"CAROLE, YOU LOOK FANTASTIC!"

"Come on in, Joyce. I was just taking the pecan pies out of the oven."

As they moved to the kitchen Joyce complained, "You've done it again—pecan pies. Oh, well, I'll diet tomorrow."

The women seated themselves at the yellow-clothed table, and Carole poured coffee for both of them.

Looking over the rim of the steaming cup, Joyce asked gently, "May I ask you what happened?"

"Of course. After all, you're my very best friend. You deserve to know. I ran away because I couldn't stand one more day of the life I was leading."

"That's no surprise," Joyce shrugged. "I could never take on the job of a pastor's wife."

"A job is exactly what it is, and I've been trying to live it full-time—with no vacations and no time off for good behavior. You see before you a reformed saint."

"And exactly what does this reformation entail?"

189

Carole leaned forward eagerly. "First, I have a job! Dr. Glynn said my old job at the bank was filled, but he offered to train me as an in-staff counselor." Mirthfully she added, "I didn't tell him how much on-the-job training I've already had. But this is the best part—they hadn't even advertised the job yet!" Her eyes danced joyfully. "I see the Lord's fingerprints all over this one."

"Good for you!" applauded her friend. "Confidentially, I thought it was a mistake for you to quit in the first place. "But," and her voice took on a note of concern, "isn't that going to keep you from participating in a lot of the activities at the church?"

Carole grinned mischievously. "Exactly. I guess I'll just have to choose my activities more carefully. I'll probably only have time for those I really am best suited for and enjoy most."

"And how does Daniel feel about all this?"

"He's delighted. He was angry when I quit because he said I was wasting some of the talents the Lord had given me."

"You have one terrific husband, Mrs. T," smiled Joyce. "And does he love you! He was absolutely frantic when I called and told him you were in Lubbock. And Leigh told everyone you had gone there to be with your sister who was critically ill."

"I also gather things didn't go too well between you and Leigh."

Carole's smile faded. "No, she made it clear she doesn't want me in the family either as Daniel's wife, or as her stepmother." She sighed. "Maybe I can eventually win her over, but it's going to take time."

"You can. No one could resist you for long."

"Your loyalty is touching—inaccurate, but touching. There are many people in the congregation I'll probably never be able to understand or count as a friend, beginning with Mrs. Charles."

"Consider yourself lucky. That would be as safe as having a pet rattlesnake in the house."

Carole had to laugh at the wisdom of Joyce's words. "Her fangs have already been shortened, I hope. The board of elders and her pastor called her in for a meeting last night. They really came down hard on gossiping. Don't you dare tell anyone I told you that," she warned.

"Discretion is my middle name."

"There's the doorbell. Help yourself to another pie. I'll be right back."

Joyce could hear Carole speaking pleasantly to her visitor. She covered her mouth with her hands to stifle her laughter as she recognized Mrs. Charles's voice at the door.

"Mrs. Thornton, I'm so glad you're back. How is your poor sister? We were all worried to death about her."

"She's doing very well. Her recovery has been amazing."

"That's nice, dear. I brought over a little cake for you, a sort of homecoming present. It's my Aunt Sophie's recipe. Been in the family for years."

"Won't you come into the living room?"

"Thank-you, dear. Is Pastor home?"

"No, he's at the church."

"Good. I mean, I wanted to talk to *you*—privately. Pastor and I had a little visit yesterday and he mentioned in passing how distressed you had been at all the gossip at the church. I just had to come by and tell you how sorry I am about all that. I'd just never forgive myself if anyone said anything that caused you a minute's worry. I told Pastor that I'd make sure those women never get a chance to say anything ugly about you while *I'm* around."

Joyce almost choked on the bite of pie she had just taken.

Carole's sweet reply floated down the hallway to her. "Why, thank-you, Mrs. Charles. I'm sure you can take care of that very nicely."

"Well, I must be going. I just had to have this little private chat with you. Be sure to return the plate, dear."

The door clicked shut and Carole walked into the kitchen to find Joyce busily drinking coffee.

"I didn't hear a word she said—honest, Carole."

"And you didn't believe any of it either, did you?" she laughed.

"That's got to be the most backhanded apology I've ever heard!"

"The part I liked best," Carole giggled, "was about her little talk with 'Pastor'. Does she honestly think that he wouldn't tell me he had talked with her? That poor woman."

"They may not have defanged her, but maybe they reduced the flow of venom. I think I'll go home now. Anything after that has to be an anti-climax. Thanks for the five pounds." She turned at the door to face Carole. "I'm glad you're back. If you ever want to scream, I'm only a phone call away. I like the new Carole."

"So do I. Good-by, dear friend. We'll get together again."

As she turned from the door, the telephone rang.

"Hello," she answered, still smiling.

"Hello, Carole, this is Leigh."

Carole had the same sensation in the pit of her stomach as when she, as a child, had ridden scary rides at the amusement park.

"Oh, I'm so sorry you missed your dad, Leigh." She was immediately on guard. "He's at the office now. Do you have that number?"

"I, uh, didn't want to speak to my dad." It all came out in a rush.

"I want to apologize for my behavior. Can you ever forgive me for all the awful things I said to you?" Leigh's words tumbled over each other. "I know I acted like a spoiled brat. I don't know if I can ever totally accept you as my mother, but I do sincerely want to try—for Dad's sake, if nothing else . . . Carole, if your letter hadn't come, I don't know what he might have done. I was so scared that you didn't love him enough to let him know where you were. It was a nightmare." She hesitated. "I almost didn't give the letter to him." A cold chill passed over Carole's heart. "But I thought it was a good-by letter, or that he would at least stop looking for you. Now I know you truly love each other and that it will be up to me to make peace with that." Her voice took on a warning note. "I'm not going to make any rash promises, but maybe we could be friends, Carole."

"Yes, I'd like that." Carole's eyes were moist. "I realize now I moved too fast. I'm sorry, too. And Leigh, if you want to—if you don't have other plans—your father and I would be so happy if you could join us for the Christmas holidays."

"I'll let you know. Thanks, Carole. And, Carole—I'm really glad Dad has you. Bye."

"Bye." Carole's eyes glistened with unshed tears. "Good-by—and hello—dear Leigh," she whispered as she hung up. She hugged herself with a fierce joy that was almost too much to bear. "Thank-you, God, oh, thank-you. I don't think I can stand another blessing from You right now. I'd die of happiness."

She didn't call Daniel. She wanted, like Mary of old, to keep these things and ponder them in her heart.

The winter wind blew cold against the stained-glass windows, but it was warm inside the sanctuary where Carole sat in her usual pew. *Funny,* she thought, *how people try to sit in the same seat each Sunday.* She watched as a visitor slipped into Prudence's usual place, and smiled as the stout woman searched frantically for another. Prudence smiled weakly at Carole when their eyes met. *She's still angry with me for dropping out of the morning ladies' group,* mused Carole. *I'll have to do something about that.* Two angry problems she wouldn't have to deal with any more were the Millers. The constant complainers had left the church. *Perhaps it's best for everyone,* she mused.

The organist began a melodic prelude. Next Sunday would be Carole's turn at the organ, and she tried to ignore the faint flutter of butterfly wings in her stomach.

She moved with the ebb and flow of the service prayerfully, particularly enjoying Daniel's sermon on Jesus as the Good Shepherd. She was acutely aware that her Shepherd was continually rescuing her from dangerous places and prodding her back into the fold.

She walked happily out of the church, visiting with the people on the way.

"Mrs. Thornton. I mean, Carole," called a smiling, chubby young woman.

"Good morning, Betsy, how are you today?"

"Fine. I wonder if you could take my Sunday school class next Sunday? We're going out of town again."

"I saw a new mother registering her daughter for classes this morning and I overheard her say she used to teach. Why don't you ask her? Her name is Sarah Herring. There's her daughter, Rachel, so she should be around here somewhere. I'm sure she can help you."

"Thanks so much. It would be nice to have a new teacher on tap. See you later."

"You handled that very neatly," said Daniel, coming up behind her. "You never did say no, and still the problem was solved. I'm going to have to watch you," he said with a gleam in his eyes. "What were you and Mr. Wilcott talking about? I haven't seen him that cheerful in months."

"I decided to make a special effort to find out why he's so grumpy all the time. He's lonely, Daniel. That's all that's wrong with him. He's really a very nice man. I think he gripes about the humor in the sermons because it gets him some attention. Do you think we might have him and Tillie over for dinner some night. Loneliness seems to be a problem for both of them."

"Wilcott and Tillie? What a match that would be! On the other hand, it might not be a bad idea. Carole, you're something else." Daniel took her arm and led her out of the church to the car.

"What are you smiling about, Carole?"

"I was just thinking what a radical change there has been in my life in the last year. I have a new husband, a new job, maybe a new daughter, and a new perspective on life."

"You sound as though you have a good grip on things."

"At least I know where the handle is. I'm learning. I'm learning."

When they arrived home, Carole served a tasty lunch which Daniel barely touched.

"I think I'll lie down for a while," he said, pushing away the plate.

"Oh, I hope you're not coming down with that flu that's going around!" she exclaimed.

Carole fluffed the pillows and settled him into bed, kissing his forehead. "You do feel warm," she worried aloud.

"My mother always kissed my forehead to take my temperature," he sighed, and closed his weary eyes.

After the worst of the flu symptoms passed, Daniel and Carole seized the opportunity of his convalescence to revel in the uninterrupted days together.

A Scrabble board lay propped up on a pillow between them on the bed. The game had been a spirited one, for Daniel was finally well on his way to complete recovery.

"Aha! A twenty-five pointer! Top that one if you can." He looked up in triumph to see Carole knock the little wooden tiles off their stand. "Darling," he said grimly, "you look like a carbon copy of me two weeks ago. I was afraid this would happen."

"I was so careful," she protested. "I disinfected everything and washed my hands a thousand times. I just can't be getting the flu." But she didn't argue as Daniel pulled the covers over her and used her own nursing methods to make her more comfortable.

"You've been overexposed this time." Sagely he added, "Just don't make any plans for the next two weeks."

The required number of days passed and still Carole's complete recovery escaped her.

"I want you to see a doctor," commanded Daniel, and promptly made the appointment for her.

The doctor's waiting room seemed littered with patients who, like Carole, hadn't been able to shake off the winter's latest strain of flu virus.

After the customary examination, Dr. Pierson startled Carole by saying, "I'd like you to run over to the hospital for a few tests." Seeing the alarm in her eyes, he added, "It's nothing to be frightened about. I just want to be sure we've covered all the bases."

When Carole relayed the instructions to Daniel, he appeared calm, but Carole noticed a tiny new worry line beside his eyes. Neither dared to speculate to the other as to the reason for the extension of Carole's medical treatment. Carole's intellect rested, while her hopeful heart prayed silently there was nothing seriously wrong with her that more rest and good food wouldn't cure.

"All right, Mrs. Thornton, that's all we need," said the medical technician. "Your doctor will call you with the results tomorrow."

As they drove home, Carole nestled beside Daniel in the car. "I'm trying to be brave, but the truth is, I'm frightened. I know God is with me," she hurried on, "but still—" the words trailed off.

Reaching over to turn on the windshield wipers, Daniel tried to clear the windows of the December drizzle that clung coldly. The hand that reached for hers was also cold, and the dark eyes that met hers lacked their customary serenity.

"Carole, my dearest heart, God never gives us more than we can bear, but," he confessed, "at this moment I am more afraid than I have ever been in my entire life."

Carole was not surprised when he turned onto the winding road that took them up to the church. There they walked through the damp mist to the door. While Daniel unlocked it, Carole's eyes swept the winter landscape. Trees locked into winter's rest stretched bare limbs to a gray sky. Even the evergreens drooped with the weight of moisture on their branches.

Daniel took her hand and led her to the front of the church where he had so persuasively proposed. They sat close to one another, fused by the uncertainty of tomorrow. What was God's plan for them?

That was the question that echoed again and again in Carole's mind as she prayed silently. *I feel so off guard, Lord,* she confessed. *You gave us to each other such a short time ago. But if I am to walk a dark valley, I thank You for giving me Daniel also to walk with me. I am trusting that Your strength will uphold us. Give us both acceptance of what is to come.*

Her eyes drifted to the familiar stained-glass window that

had inspired her so many times before. The Savior's face was dimly lit from the gray light outside. The colors may have been less brilliant, but Carole felt a gentle peace glowing in her heart. She turned to Daniel. His eyes were lifted to the window and they were misted with tears, but his smile told her that he, too, had put their lives once again into God's hands. Gently he folded her into his arms and held her for a long moment.

As they left the church, Carole saw the winter as a time of promise, not the dead dreams of summer. A certainty grew within her that she would share the spring with Daniel.

They sat before a crackling fire the next day while Daniel read and Carole worked the crossword puzzle from the daily paper. Carole plumped up the pillows behind her and thought how odd it was that the phone had not rung a single time since they had been home. *The Lord must be holding all our calls until the most important one comes in*, she mused. She didn't even start when suddenly it *did* ring, piercing the stillness.

Daniel and Carole looked at each other for a split second, unsure as to which of them should take the call. Carole made the choice. "Hello," she said calmly. "Yes, Dr. Pierson." Gingerly she lowered herself into the chair beside the phone table. Daniel rose and swiftly walked over to sit beside her, eyes fastened anxiously on her face. "Yes, I can hear you perfectly. Yes. You're sure?" The expression on her face was frozen. "There's absolutely no chance that you might be wrong?" Daniel leaned forward in a futile attempt to hear what was being said on the other end of the line. "Yes, I will. Thank-you, Doctor." Shakily she tried to replace the phone in its holder.

"Well?" demanded an almost breathless Daniel.

Her eyes were glazed with disbelief as she looked down

over the months stretching out before her. With great difficulty she focused her eyes on Daniel's frantic face. "I'm going to have a child."

She spoke so softly that Daniel was sure he had not heard correctly. "What? What did you say?"

"I'm going to have a child. It's impossible, but I'm going to have a child!" she almost shouted. Joy blazed across her features, lighting them with an ethereal beauty. For a second she thought she might faint with happiness. Had she fainted she would never have hit the floor, for Daniel swept her hard against his broad chest and was holding her tightly. They stood locked together in the embrace until Carole felt Daniel's tears mingle with her own, tracing a happy path down their faces.

"Dear Lord," Daniel prayed, "we thank You for this miracle, and we ask forgiveness for any doubts we may have had about Your love for us. Thank You, God," he whispered against Carole's mouth as he brushed her lips with his. "Thank You, for the gift of a child, and for my Morning Song."

## About the Author

It is not surprising that **Linda Timian Herring** is the wife of a Lutheran minister. She and her husband have churches in Monahans and Kermit, Texas, where she also teaches. She is the mother of four grown children. Her writing has become another avenue of ministry whereby she both entertains and uplifts with her down-to-earth view of Christianity.

Forever Romances are inspirational romances designed to bring you a joyful, heart-lifting reading experience. If you would like more information about joining our Forever Romance book series, please write to us:

Guideposts Customer Service
39 Seminary Hill Road
Carmel, NY 10512

Forever Romances are chosen by the same staff that prepares *Guideposts,* a monthly magazine filled with true stories of people's adventures in faith. *Guideposts* is not sold on the newsstand. It's available by subscription only. And subscribing is easy. Write to the address above and you can begin reading *Guideposts* soon. When you subscribe, each month you can count on receiving exciting new evidence of God's Presence, His Guidance and His limitless love for all of us.